*Leopard's Prey*

ALSO BY LEONARD WIBBERLEY

# *The Treegate Chronicles*

JOHN TREEGATE'S MUSKET
PETER TREEGATE'S WAR
SEA CAPTAIN FROM SALEM
TREEGATE'S RAIDERS

LEONARD WIBBERLEY

# Leopard's Prey

AN ARIEL BOOK

FARRAR, STRAUS AND GIROUX
NEW YORK

G345251

Library of Congress catalog card
number: 78-149225
SBN 374.3.4378.0
First printing, 1971
Published simultaneously in Canada
by Doubleday Canada Ltd., Toronto
Printed in the United States of America
Designed by Millicent Fairhurst

*Leopard's Prey*

# 1

"AND I say confound the French," said Mr. Peter Treegate and he brought his big fist down on the table before
him so that that stout piece of mahogany shuddered under
the blow. "The French are a perfidious, petty, self-serving,
vain, devious, rapacious and venal nation. I have met three
good Frenchmen in my lifetime. That was in the Yorktown campaign—and they were all three of them dead."

"They were our allies in that war, sir," said the Reverend Broome, who was seated halfway down the table.
"Indeed," he added, toying with the glass of wine before
him, "I am not sure that the French were not then our
saviors. If de Grasse had not bottled up Cornwallis at
Yorktown, who knows what the outcome might have
been?"

"We would still have been the victors, and that for a
reason which must be obvious to you gentlemen who,
whatever our callings, know something of the sea," said

3

Mr. Treegate. "No nation can long support a war fought at three thousand miles' distance from the homeland, for the problems of supply and of communication are insoluble. When the British Redcoat fires a round at the King's enemies in Europe, that shot may cost His Majesty a shilling. But when he fires a round at the King's enemies in America, let us say, then the cost is likely to be closer to a pound.

"Such costs cannot long be borne. We would have had our victory in that war without the French, though it might have been a little delayed."

The discussion was taking place in the dining room of the Treegate house at Salem, Massachusetts. The year was 1807 and the occasion was the fiftieth birthday of Mr. Peter Treegate, onetime frontiersman and organizer of Treegate's Raiders during the Revolutionary War. He was now a prosperous importer and exporter of Salem, being principal proprietor of the firm of Treegate and Manly, which had offices and warehouses in Boston and New York as well as Salem, and agents in half a dozen posts about the world.

The room was richly furnished. The table and chairs were of the best West Indian mahogany, polished with beeswax. There were Turkey carpets on the floor, and the drapes on the eight-foot windows, which led out onto a wrought-iron balcony overlooking an extensive lawn and garden, were of blue London plush edged with silver tassels.

A fireplace in one wall of the room had a white marble mantelpiece by the Adam brothers, supported on the two

4

sides by sea nymphs reaching upward out of marble surf. On the center of the mantelpiece was a clock under a glass dome, constructed according to Halley's principles, and one which required winding only every eight days. Mr. Treegate affirmed (and his wife denied) that it was a better timekeeper than the old Salem grandfather clock which ticked solemnly in its corner to the side and announced on a dial set in the clock face the phases of the moon. There were two large mahogany cabinets, glass-fronted, in which were kept the best dishes of the household and, between these, pinned to the wall, a Great Sword or claymore such as was used until recently by the Scottish Highlanders. Beside it were half a dozen tomahawks of Shawnee, Mohawk, Iroquois and Cherokee manufacture. These items, so much at odds with the other furnishings of the room, told of the younger days of Mr. Treegate, spent among the Indians and the Scots settlers in the Blue Ridge and Appalachian Mountains.

Although dinner was over, the ladies were still present at the table, for Mr. Treegate did not follow the London style of dismissing them to the withdrawing room so that the men could be at their ease over their wine. Mrs. Treegate, mild and grey-haired, and dressed somewhat plainly in a gown of pale green, sat at the opposite end of the table from her husband and served a dish of coffee to those who preferred this to wine. Overhearing her husband, she hoped to head off the talk from foreign affairs, on which he always grew forcible, but it was Mrs. Abigail Adams from Braintree, the wife of the former President, who came to her rescue.

5

"The coffee is delicious, Mrs. Treegate," she said. "Tell me, is it Dutch or Portuguese in origin?"

"Why, Portuguese, madam," said Mrs. Treegate. "It comes from the Brazils. I think myself the Arabian is best, but it is scarcely to be come by now." Mrs. Adams was tactful enough not to inquire the reason, lest this lead back in some manner to Mr. Treegate's view on the French, and the conversation was eased into more tranquil channels—the superiority of the wild rice of the Carolinas over the new Italian strains; the extension of the system of canals, which was greatly speeding up the transportation of goods between the States; and the effect on world trade of Mr. Robert Fulton's remarkable steamboat, which was now plying between New York and Albany and on which Mrs. Broome, wife of the Reverend Broome, had taken a trip that summer.

"I was frightened every moment of the journey," she asserted. "The heat from the furnace was dreadful, and such a prodigious emission of smoke and sparks you never did see. I was very glad to get off it, I assure you."

"How long did the voyage last?" asked Mrs. Adams.

"I should think six hours," said Mrs. Broome. "I could not pronounce it enjoyable. It was an ordeal, like spending the afternoon in close proximity to a dragon. That form of travel has little to recommend it, I assure you. Although I wore a pinafore and a cloak over my gown, it was most dreadfully spotted with smuts from the funnel. I would not venture on such an expedition again."

"And how about you, Mrs. Treegate?" said Mrs. Adams. "Would you try such a voyage?"

6

Mrs. Treegate glanced down the length of the table at her husband, as if to get from him what answer she should make. But he was engaged with a Colonel of Militia. Thrown back on her own resources, she said, "I do not know, but if Mr. Treegate required me to make the voyage, then I would make it."

Mrs. Adams laughed. "You give a proper example to us all at a time when I confess wives become too forward," she said, and Nancy Treegate blushed and excused herself to see about the dessert, which seemed delayed. She returned in a few moments with a vast plum pudding covered with a custard sauce, which was set down before Mr. Treegate.

"The children," she said.

"Huh?" he asked, a little bemused, for he had been explaining to the Colonel of Militia, who had applied for a transfer to Kaskakia on the Ohio, that the Shawnee were now the leading Indian nation on the frontier and the one which had to be watched.

"The children," said Mrs. Treegate. "You promised they could come in for the dessert."

"Ah, yes," said Mr. Treegate. "Are they ready?"

"Yes," said his wife.

"Are young Manly's ears washed?"

"Yes," said his wife, repressing a smile. "I washed them myself."

"And his hair? There was tar in it the last time I saw him."

"It is brushed," said his wife.

"What did you do about the tar?"

7

"I got it out—with butter."

This strange method of removing tar caused Mr. Treegate to exchange a mystified glance with the Colonel. "All right," he said to his wife, "bring them in. But they are to be quiet and listen to their elders."

Mrs. Treegate nodded to one of the servants. Mr. Treegate rose, tapped his wine glass to get the attention of his guests, and said, "Ladies and Gentlemen: As many of you know, it has been my custom for some years to have the younger generation of Treegates share dessert with me on my birthday. They demand this privilege now, and I trust you will bear with me while I indulge them."

There were smiles of pleasure and a little ripple of applause around the table and the adults turned aside from the table somewhat ponderously in their chairs to welcome the newcomers. The vast double doors of golden oak at the end of the room were opened and four children, thoroughly scrubbed, dressed in their best and headed by a boy of thirteen, entered. They were in some awe at so large a compnay of adults, and in any case they were allowed into this room only twice a year—on Mr. Treegate's birthday and at Christmas—so the very place alone tended to subdue them. The boldest was the older boy, who walked without hesitation ahead of the others, evading the restraining hand of the servant.

He had long fair hair, with a touch of red in it, which was gathered in the fashion of the time, in a queue behind his neck. His eyes were blue-grey and had a direct look to them; his chin was firm, and his nose would have been a firm straight line had it not been broken and poorly reset.

He was dressed in the pantaloons of the time, which revealed an inch or two of multicolored stocking above his shoes, and a cutaway coat of deep blue with flaring lapels of buff. His chin was thrust upward by a vast stock.

When the boy had come within a few feet of the table, he turned to Mr. Treegate and said clearly and firmly, "Happy birthday, Uncle." And then, addressing himself to the general company, said clearly, "Ladies and Gentlemen. My compliments."

The assurance of the boy rather took the company aback, but Mrs. Abigail Adams remarked to her neighbor, behind her fan, "More like his uncle than his father in every respect."

Mr. Treegate eyed the boy with a measure of pride and surprise. "Thank you," he said. "If you'll bide your time for a moment, I will make the introductions." The boy blushed slightly at the rebuke and Mr. Treegate continued.

"Ladies and gentlemen, allow me to present the younger generation of the Treegates. My nephew, Master Manly Treegate"—the boy bowed again. "My niece, Mistress Prudence Treegate"—a girl of ten in an unhooped dress of blue taffeta made a curtsy. "My niece, Nancy, and my nephew, Godspeace Treegate." The two tiny children bobbed to the company from the vicinity of the door, the boy called Godspeace holding his sister's hand so as to bring her down at the right time and up at the right time as he had been instructed by his grandmother.

"And now, madam," said Mr. Treegate, turning to his wife, "if there is a table for the children, I will cut this great pudding and they can be served." Immediately there was a hum of dissent from among the guests, who in this way made it clear that they wanted the children sitting with them and not at a separate table.

Lest Mr. Treegate should miss this point, Abigail Adams got the two girls and brought them to the table herself, remarking that she had several grandchildren of her own and that she was happy to say that they were all thoroughly spoiled. "Which," she added, "is my doing, and indeed my privilege."

The Colonel of Foot (his name was Beddington) made room immediately for young Manly Treegate to sit by his huge uncle, who was by far the tallest man in the room. The uncle cut slices of the pudding, which gave off the most delicious aroma of plums, ginger and raisins, and the children had soon monopolized the attention of the guests.

That question which is put inevitably by adults to children was now put by young Colonel Beddington (a man of little imagination but solid sense) to young Manly Treegate. "Well," he said, "what are you going to be when you grow up?"

"A sea captain," said the boy. "Like Grandfather Manly." The Colonel looked puzzled. He was new to the area, coming indeed from New York, and spoke with the slow, almost rolling accent of the people of that city.

"He means my father-in-law, Peace of God Manly," said Peter Treegate. "He commanded the brig *Nancy* in the War of Revolution and was a raider for some time off the English coast. It was he who brought back the news of the peace."

Colonel Beddington nodded. "I remember now," he said. "A sea captain, eh? Well, your uncle has no doubt enough ships to give you both training and command. How many have you now, Mr. Treegate—in round numbers."

"Fourteen in all," said Peter Treegate. "But my partners and I charter perhaps half a dozen more when some particular cargo requires to be moved. The India and China trades are coming on well, as you perhaps know. But we shall not have a real trade with the Orient until we have a harbor on the Pacific Coast and a good overland route for shipping goods."

"I take leave to doubt that there will ever be such a route, sir," said Colonel Beddington. "The report brought back by Lewis and Clark was not conducive to optimism."

Mr. Treegate grunted. "There is a Spanish trail, going through Santa Fe—so I have heard," he said. "It is used for transporting goods by mule and, I believe, in wagons of a kind. Such a trail as that would serve us handily."

Manly Treegate had stopped eating his plum pudding and was studying his uncle's face.

"Spanish is for Spain," said Colonel Beddington dryly.

"America is for Americans," said Mr. Treegate. "I don't know by what means it will come about, sir, but there is room on this continent for only one power. We have pushed or bought the French out. Spain must go next. And what is here must be ours."

Beddington looked sharply at Mr. Treegate and said, "I can tell you this as an Army man. Mr. Jefferson will not hear of force. Why, sir, the Army is cut to the size of a corporal's guard. There are enough of us to deal with the Indians only provided the Indians do not unite. As for the Navy—well, you know better than I what is happening there. A few sloops of war and brigs authorized and our big frigates laid up or lacking crews, and nothing building but gunboats. A hundred of them, I hear, have been ordered or are to be ordered. A hundred barges that have to be towed here and there and must send their guns below in rough weather lest they capsize.

"There's a Navy for you. And we with the biggest seacoast in the civilized world to protect and all our commerce dependent on sea trade."

"I have heard," said Mr. Treegate, "that one of Mr. Jefferson's gunboats was blown in the winter gales half a mile ashore and some wit remarked that, though we have not the best Navy afloat, we can certainly claim the best Navy on earth."

Beddington laughed and Manly Treegate looked squarely at his uncle and said, "Do you think, sir, that we must fight the Spanish?"

"I think your ears are too big and if we fight anybody it must be the French," said his uncle.

"I would differ on that," said Colonel Beddington. "It is the Redcoats I fear. And with the Navy but a wreck and the Army a threadbare coat, there are times, sir, when I find it hard to sleep at nights."

# 2

When the dinner guests had all left and the great dining room had been cleared, Peter Treegate withdrew to his study to look over some invoices recently arrived from Fractor and Sims, his British agents at Bristol, and compare them with his own records. His company had prospered remarkably during the French and English war which the world was to know as the Napoleonic War. There was a demand in both England and France for almost every kind of merchandise, and though the risks to shipping were high, the profits were even higher. Indeed, the whole of the American shipping business was enjoying a prosperity which was certain to last as long as the war lasted.

To be sure, it was necessary for the Treegate ships, and all others venturing on the high seas, to get a certificate from the Royal Britannic Navy giving them freedom of

13

passage. But such certificates were not difficult to obtain, and a wise shipowner got a similar certificate from the French naval authorities. This technically prevented seizure of the vessel, though there were British and French captains, greedy for personal gain, who would pretend that a certificate was not in order and seize a vessel in any case. But this was an exception. The plain fact of the matter was that, with France trying to starve Britain, and Britain trying to starve France, both nations were anxious for American goods and dared not prey too heavily on American vessels on the high seas.

When Peter Treegate had said that there were fourteen ships flying the house flag of Treegate and Manly (which showed a red tomahawk on a green background), he had not included half a dozen smaller vessels engaged in the coasting trade. His problem was not ships but men to man them. The British had started the game of stopping American vessels on the high seas and taking off their crews, and the French had followed suit. If a seaman had an accent which a boarding officer pronounced English, Irish, Scots or Welsh (and such accents were common throughout the United States), he was pronounced a deserter and taken on board the British vessel. Against this seizure of men, there was no redress, and Peter Treegate, sitting down over his accounts in his study, was concerned also that many of his ships were too lightly manned to handle the heavy autumn weather ahead.

He smoothed the sheaf of invoices on the desk before him and glanced at the heading. The shipment, it was announced in beautiful handwriting, was off the scow

*Enterprise* and the brig *Huron,* and the cargo of the *Enterprise* had consisted of fifteen hundred hogsheads of Virginia tobacco, fifty tons of New England rumbullion of the second grade, two bales of bison hides and four more of beaver furs, as well as ten crates of what was described as "miscellaneous stuffs." That of the brig was similar, though in place of rum there was substituted French wines. This represented a two-way trade of some hazard—buying wines in France, shipping them to America, and then, with a British Navy certificate, reshipping them to England, where the direct purchase of wine from France was of course impossible since the two countries were at war with each other.

Having glanced over the general description of the cargo, Mr. Treegate was about to go into the details on the following pages when he heard a somewhat cautious knock on his study door. Irritated, he ignored it, whereupon it was repeated after a little while, and somewhat more boldly.

"Who is it?" he cried. "Come in."

The door was opened and his nephew Manly appeared. Mr. Treegate had mixed feelings about the boy, whose care he had undertaken, together with his brother and sisters, on the death of their father in a smallpox epidemic two years before. At times he felt the boy was a fine young fellow who would make his way readily in the world. At times he felt the boy was flighty and unstable, quick-tempered and headstrong, and must certainly come to ruin.

Peter Treegate had no children of his own, though

married twenty-six years. This was one of the conditions of life which he found hard to bear. He had thought of adopting Manly and the other children but had not done so, delaying because of some obscure reason which he could not quite fathom. He told himself that the children were entitled to their true father's identity. But the fact was that, although the children were his brother's, he was hurt that he had none of his own and, in his hurt, kept a little distance between himself and them.

"Well," said Peter Treegate as his nephew stood in the doorway. "What do you want?" He was immediately disturbed to find himself speaking so sharply to the boy, but had no remedy for this, for gentleness did not come readily to him.

"Sir," said the boy, "Mrs. Treegate tells me that you are intending journeying to Norfolk, Virginia, tomorrow."

"So?"

The boy hesitated. The object of the interview was being arrived at too summarily and he knew from past experience that this inevitably meant refusal.

"The school term is over, sir," said the boy, mentioning a fact which only the womenfolk ever seemed to remember. "I was hoping that I could accompany you. I could help with the baggage should we go by coach, and should we go by horseback I could manage the stabling of the animals while you are away on any particular business." He paused and added, "I am accounted good with horses, sir. Also, a journey to Virginia would help to further my education."

Despite himself, Peter Treegate smiled. This was an old

gambit. Whenever a young fellow wished to do anything pleasurable, he pleaded it would further his education and the very word "education" was thought to have some kind of magic, excusing expense and horrendous wastages of time.

"So the school is out," said Treegate. "Yes. I recall Reverend Broome's making that remark at dinner, and with some relief. And what was your achievement in Latin grammar?"

"Sixty-five percent, sir," said the boy.

"You have some excuse for so miserable a performance?"

"No, sir."

"You have a reason?"

"Yes, sir."

"And what is it?"

"I detest Latin," said the boy firmly and without hesitation. "I find it without sense or application."

"The very fact that you detest Latin should make you apply yourself to it all the harder," said Mr. Treegate. "Surely you realize that there is little virtue in being good at that which you enjoy?"

The boy made no reply. He was becoming quite familiar with this particular lecture, which was usually the preface to being denied what he was asking for. He eyed his uncle, whose vast frame made the desk before him seem but a table. His uncle, he decided, was undoubtedly the strongest man in Massachusetts, and perhaps even in New Hampshire, though he had heard that there was a General Sullivan in New Hampshire who had wrestled a bear. His father had not been so big a man. He loved his father, but for his uncle he reserved a place among the heroes and thought that his name should have been not Peter but Ajax.

His uncle went on with the lecture. The improvement of man depended entirely on self-discipline. Animals were unable to discipline themselves and so had to be punished to make them perform particular tasks. Man alone could discipline himself and, by so doing, improve himself as a person and make a contribution to the improvement of society as a whole. Furthermore, the world extracted a terrible penalty from those who had no self-discipline. That penalty was rejection and poverty and failure in the eyes of one's fellows.

The boy's eyes strayed from his uncle's grim face to a long-barreled, heavy musket that was fixed to the wall behind his uncle's desk. That musket had belonged to his grandfather—his paternal grandfather, John Treegate. He had carried it at the Battle of Abraham Heights, fought for the liberation of Canada from what his uncle called the "perfidious French." And his grandfather had used the same musket at Bunker Hill for the liberation of the Colonies from what some of his friends called "the perfidious English." It was old-fashioned now, but he had heard his uncle say he could bring down a black squirrel with it at two hundred yards.

". . . and I assure you, young Manly," his uncle said, "that Latin is far more educational than Virginia, and you will have more profit from studying Cicero than from holding a horse's head on the Norfolk quays."

Manly realized that he would not be allowed to accompany his uncle, but he was not one to give up easily. Furthermore, he had a temper, and in his disappointment it now came to the surface. "Sir," he said, "you are not fair."

"What do you mean by that, you young cub?" Peter Treegate demanded.

"You are not fair in that you want my schooling to continue all summer. There should be a time when I don't have to think of Latin."

"Do you dare to stand there and question my decision?" demanded Mr. Treegate.

"I do not question your decision, sir," said the boy firmly. "But I have a right to speak for myself."

"Out of here before I lose my temper," said his uncle, and the boy, with a stiff hostile bow, went, closing the door with something like a slam. Mr. Treegate was still staring at it when there came another knock. "Who is it now?" he demanded, and the door opened and his wife Nancy entered.

"Madam," said Mr. Treegate. "I am, as you see, busy with my accounts."

"I shall not interrupt you with as much as a word, Mr. Treegate," said his wife. She sat quietly in a chair, her hands in her lap. Mr. Treegate grunted and turned to his invoices. But though he tried to immerse himself in hundredweights of salted cod, and pipes of white Burgundy and bails of cotton batting, the silent presence of his wife intruded itself. In the end he turned to her in exasperation.

"Madam," he said. "If you would speak I would answer you. But how am I to answer silence? What is it you want?"

"Mr. Treegate, I do not wish to intrude upon your work," said his wife. "I am quite content to remain here until you have done all that you think is necessary."

"I am quite unable to do all that I think is necessary while you remain here."

"In that case I will leave, Mr. Treegate," said his wife. But her husband realized that this would worsen rather than improve the situation.

"Tell me what brings you here," he demanded.

"I think you are being unfair to Manly and unfair to yourself," she replied. "You should permit him to go with you. You should allow yourself more of his company."

"Would you reward slack work at school—downright idleness, in fact—with a pleasant excursion by horseback of several hundred miles?" asked her husband.

"Mr. Treegate," said his wife, "the boy needs a man's company. He is too much with women and younger children."

"He needs to tend to his schooling."

"Mr. Treegate, when you were his age, you were not at your books."

This was true. At the boy's age Peter Treegate had been living in the wilderness of the Carolinas, with his foster father, the fierce Maclaren of Spey. He had been learning the wisdom of the wilderness rather than the wisdom of Rome. For a second he smelled the pine resin in the hot sun and glimpsed the blue mountain air and the stern face of the Maclaren of Spey, whom he had had in the end to desert.

"You speak of events of almost forty years ago, madam," he said.

"Nonetheless, it was the frontier and the company of men which gave you your strength," said Mrs. Treegate. "The boy has an equal need."

"Did he set you to this?"

"No. He begged me not to interfere."

"What did he say—precisely."

"He said he would not go anywhere—in any man's company—where he was not welcome."

"He did, eh?" said Peter Treegate, ruffled at the answer. "Well, tell him he is to prepare to accompany me to Virginia whether he wishes it or not. And he had better be in good shape, for, madam, I will ride a hundred miles a day and perhaps more. And now you may retire."

"I will wait until you have finished your accounts," said his wife.

"Then you must fall asleep there, for they cannot wait until tomorrow," said her husband. "You would do better to go to bed." But she remained. Two hours later, when the candles were all but spent, he arose from the desk and, picking up his sleeping wife tenderly, carried her to bed.

# 3

NORFOLK proved a city of marvels out of some exotic tale for Manly Treegate. The air was soft and warm and had in midsummer a heady fragrance of both sea and land—a mixture of ozone and magnolia which seemed to the boy the very air of heaven. Water and city he found marvelously intermingled, so that at times he turned a corner and found before him not another street but a wide expanse of river and, floating on it, ketches and wherries laden with cargo. Salem was his home town, and the long neck of harbor which plunged into the city dominated the place. But Norfolk he found far more of a "water city" than Salem. It was of good size, having, his uncle said, been burned down to the ground during the Revolution almost thirty years before. Only St. Paul's Church was saved, and the burning had been done at the instigation of Lord Dunmore, the British governor of Virginia. The city was new then, scarcely thirty years old, which was a marvel in itself, for Salem was old—close to two hundred years old and all of stone.

A great number of the people in the streets were blacks—slaves, his uncle said—and, there being no slaves in Salem, though the town had grown fat on the trade, the boy watched them with interest. They seemed listless and idle and quickly took on a mock servility when spoken to by their masters. But he had expected chains and saw none, and the slaves seemed to be free to roam about and gather together and gossip in little groups.

"They are very largely useless," said Mr. Treegate. "The greater number of them study from childhood to do as little as possible and that as badly as it may be done. They might as well be set free."

"Then why are they not freed, sir?" asked Manly.

"In the greater number of cases it would be a hardship on them. Free, without a trade, without land, without education, they could not earn enough to feed themselves and their children. There are exceptions, but they are few. Come with me and I will introduce you to one such exception."

The two, during their conversation, were walking down one of the many wharves that lined the bay. The wharf was paved with cobblestones, as were most of the principal streets of Norfolk, the cobbles being used to bear the weight of the heavy drays which rumbled and slithered over them constantly. When such a dray passed, conversation was quite impossible, such was the thunderous noise of the iron-tired wheels on the cobbles, the clattering of the great horse's hoofs, and above this the staccato crack of the drayman's whip. Two such drays passed now—one laden with hogsheads of tobacco for shipment to England, and the other with sacks of wheat flour for what Mr. Treegate called a "port of opportunity." He did not explain the phrase.

They crossed the cobbled area of the wharf where ten such drays could be placed side by side and, passing a group of warehouses from whose vast dark interiors came the aroma of hides and tobacco, of salted fish and rum and cottonseed oil, they went down a side street whose surface was entirely paved with crushed oyster shells. From here they turned off into a small alley at the back of one of the great blocks of warehouses and found, on one side, among a number of inferior wooden dwellings, one which was larger than all its fellows. It stood behind a picket fence which had been tarred to preserve it from the weather, and there was a low gate in the fence with a signboard announcing:

*T. Jones*
*Factor*

Mr. Treegate examined this sign with some affection and then, throwing open the gate, walked in and pulled with vigor on a bell rope which stood before the sunbeaten door of the house. They were not admitted immediately. Instead, a small shutter in the door opened and a pair of eyes stared for a moment directly at Mr. Treegate and then, with some difficulty because of the angle involved, at Manly Treegate.

Not a word was said, and this scrutiny took an uncomfortably long time. At last the little shutter was snapped shut and, after some fumbling with bolts and locks, the door was opened. Manly had rarely seen such a massive door. On the outside, it seemed ordinary, but now he saw it was six inches thick and studded with vast iron spikes and crosspieces, so that it could scarcely be broken apart with a battering ram.

"Well, Peggott," said Mr. Treegate when they were inside. "I am happy to see you have not forgotten me."

"Never likely to," said Peggott dourly. He shifted his look to Manly and said, "Who is the young 'un?"

"My nephew, Manly Treegate," said Mr. Treegate. "Shake hands with Mr. Peggott." The man reached out a big square hand to Manly. He was short in stature, with shoulders that were broad and tremendously strong.

The exterior of the house had been shabby and the interior matched its condition. The wooden floor of the corridor in which they stood was bare and scrubbed, and a flight of narrow stairs, served by a wobbly banister, led to an upper landing.

"He's upstairs," said Mr. Peggott. "You can go straight up. He's expecting you." Having said this, Mr. Peggott placed his broad back against the door as if to reinforce the bars and locks with which it was already stoutly fastened. Manly was surprised to note that he had a pistol of two barrels thrust in his waistband, and indeed there was about Mr. Peggott, now that he examined him closely, a certain piratical air.

"Are you expecting callers?" asked Mr. Treegate.

"There's two squadrons in the bay and a frigate of our own," said Mr. Peggott. "Stand by to repel boarders would be seamanly, I'd say."

Mr. Treegate nodded and started up the stairs without another word. At the top was a landing going to left and right, along the wings of the house. He turned to the left and, passing two doors, knocked lightly on the third and entered without further ado.

Manly found himself in a large room which provided an astonishing contrast to the rest of the house, for it was sumptuously furnished. There was a thick blue carpet on the floor and heavy drapes to match hung on the windows. A chandelier with a thousand glistening points of light hung from the ceiling, and there were several easy chairs about, with full high backs covered in what he recognized from his uncle's home as fine French petit-point embroidery. There was a fireplace of white marble to one side, which, the weather being warm, was filled with masses of pink roses. The fire irons and guard rail were of gleaming brass. At the side of the room, which overlooked the street, were two long windows and, between these, to take the fullest advantage of the light, a small elegant desk such as a lady might have in her boudoir, the legs shaped in graceful curves and the edges of the top decorated by golden fretwork. Seated at the desk was a black man who jumped up with such alacrity when they entered that Manly thought for a moment he had been caught seated in his master's chair.

"Mr. Treegate," cried he, coming forward with one hand outstretched and making an elaborate show of avoiding the furniture in his anxiety to hurry to his visitor. "Always a delight to see you, sir. Always a delight. I heard you were in Norfolk and hoped you would call on me." He turned and, pretending to catch sight of Manly, said, "And who is this fine young gentleman? He has your look, Mr. Treegate. He has your look without a doubt."

"My nephew, Manly Treegate," said the other. "And this is Mr. Theophilous Jones—Factor."

Manly, too surprised to utter a word, shook hands. Theophilous Jones was the first blackamoor he had met. The contrast between this dapper, brisk, urbane man and the listless slaves in the streets of Norfolk was overwhelming. Mr. Theophilous Jones was small, almost foppish in his dress, and his whole face was alight with humor and intelligence. His uncle and Mr. Jones, having exchanged a few pleasantries in which the latter inquired earnestly after the health of Mrs. Treegate, were soon engaged in business. Their talk left Manly puzzled. The conversation concerned ships and sailing dates and cargoes, and seemingly certain seasonal perils of the sea. Mr. Jones, for instance, cautioned Mr. Treegate to avoid the Ushant landfall in October and November.

"Inbound, Charleston will be open from the third of October on," he said. "And Mystic will always be safe if New York is cleared by fifty miles in the approach. The Jersey coast is not to be thought of until January, and there will be a French flavor to the Delaware estuary through the whole of December."

"Your intelligence is sound in all these particulars?" asked Mr. Treegate.

27

"I will insure the cargoes in whatever amount you require," said Mr. Jones, and Manly guessed then that he was an underwriter of goods in the sea trade.

"I have *Speedwell* and *Prudence* expected from London, and *Salem Trader* is three weeks overdue from the French islands," said Mr. Treegate. "You carry the papers on all those, you know."

"I do indeed, and it is a great privilege," said Mr. Jones. *"Speedwell* was off the Portuguese islands four weeks ago and is probably making a slow passage in the trades. *Prudence* was delayed by foul weather off the Head of Kinsale and had to put back with some damage to her gear. But this will not delay her more than a week, I fancy. *Salem Trader* will make the Hampton Roads tonight."

Then there was some discussion of cargoes and wagon transport in which Manly was little interested, though he wondered what kind of wood sandalwood might be and where the Fiji Islands were which were mentioned as a new and prolific source of it. But he pricked up his ears a few sentences later when Mr. Jones said, in an offhand manner, that there was both a French and a British naval force in Chesapeake Bay not far from Norfolk and that the United States frigate *Chesapeake* was also in the bay and had orders to sail for France.

"She is to leave on the afternoon tide," said Mr. Jones. He took a handsome gold watch from the fob pocket of his immaculate buckskin breeches and examined it. "In fact, I would say she left an hour ago. And the significance of that, for you and me, Mr. Treegate, is that this evening there will not be a sailor to be found in Norfolk or within twenty miles of the town. Of course," he added, "as you know, I am always prepared for such situations and your ships will not suffer. Hands will be available."

"I have heard, since coming to town, of desertions from the British ships," said Mr. Treegate with a smile.

"Oh, no doubt such things happen," said Mr. Jones innocently. "It is a hard thing indeed to prevent a poor seaman from improving his lot if the opportunity offers. King and country are sacred, of course. But then, after fifteen years of impressed service, many wonder whether king and country are that valuable and whether it would not be nice to transfer allegiance—the pay and working conditions being advantageous."

"Has the sailing of *Chesapeake* got anything to do with Peggott standing before the door below, armed like a buccaneer?" asked Mr. Treegate.

Instead of answering right away, Mr. Jones rose and went to the elegant marble mantelpiece over the fireplace and took from it a snuffbox of old ivory. He opened the lid and inhaled a substantial pinch of snuff in each nostril. The snuff was so strong that in a few seconds tears were glistening in his eyes and indeed streaming down his cheeks, which seemed to give him pleasure, for he offered the snuffbox to Mr. Treegate and to Manly.

"Peggott is a nervous fellow," he said, "and has been standing in that way ever since he heard that *Chesapeake* is to sail. He feels that, with the departure of the protection of our own frigate, His Majesty is likely to send a shore party looking for missing seamen."

"Of whom, of course, he is one," said Mr. Treegate.

"Was one," said Mr. Jones. "Fifteen years on the gun deck, he says, shipped from one vessel to another and never allowed to land in all that time. I assure you, my good friend, I found slavery infinitely preferable. At least I had firm ground under my feet and some prospect of buying my release. But it is not entirely for himself that Peggott is worried. He has had his ears clipped and the corners of his nostrils shaped so few would recognize him now, while his accent, after much practice, is good Yankee. No. Peggott is concerned about me."

"You?" echoed Mr. Treegate. "I thought all that menaced you lay in Haiti."

"Oh, no," said Theophilous Jones. "I hardly give a thought to Haiti now. But among the—well, the deserters —from the British squadron is a highly valued bosun by the name of Jenkin Ratford. He is a man of more than ordinary intelligence and he in fact organized a large-scale desertion which I was able to assist as a result of certain influences I have among the watermen and wherry crews."

"How many?" asked Mr. Treegate.

"A dozen in all, including three topmast hands who claim to be Americans anyway."

Mr. Treegate glanced at his nephew. "I think you might take a short turn down the corridor, Manly," he said.

"Not at all. Not at all," said Mr. Jones. "He is plainly a gentleman and the son of a gentleman. And among gentlemen there is no such thing as a violated confidence.

In any case, I was able to find a very safe berth for bosun Ratford."

"As an inland drover?" asked Mr. Treegate.

"Oh, no. The man's an excellent seaman. His talents would be entirely wasted on land. I found him a berth afloat."

"Good heavens," cried Mr. Treegate. "Afloat! I shouldn't think any berth afloat would be safe for a deserter from a British warship," said Mr. Treegate.

"You are mistaken," said Mr. Jones. "There is one berth afloat which is completely safe for such a man. Bosun Ratford, formerly of His Majesty's frigate *Leopard,* is at this moment sailing down the bay as a bosun on the United States frigate *Chesapeake.* And that is one ship, I assure you, that the British would not dare to stop and search."

He extended the snuffbox to Mr. Treegate. "An excellent piece," he said. "It is a gift from Bosun Ratford, made, he assures me, from a beef bone found in a cask of salt horse while serving aboard *Leopard.* A unique mark of gratitude and one I shall treasure."

# 4

COMMODORE James Barron, flying his broad riband from the mainmast trunk of the United States frigate *Chesapeake,* caught the early tide down Chesapeake Bay that morning. Anxious to clear the land and get a true breeze for Europe before sundown, he was in a hurry to get away and in no good temper, for stores had been arriving through the night and were still arriving half an hour before he gave the order for the anchor to be weighed.

Several packing cases were still to come, he had been told, and he cursed the latitude of the Navy Department which turned a fighting frigate into a freighter in the service of citizens with influence. His main deck and his gun decks were covered with piles of miscellaneous cargo —some of it the ship's and some of it privately owned— which had yet to be stowed. His crew, handling sheets and braces to swing the big yards to the wind and trim them right, were dodging shoulder-high among bales and parcels and crates. Worse, all this fumbling and stumbling was going on under the eyes of both the French and the British squadrons in the bay, who had their glasses trained on him.

The anchor was hardly up and the topsail yards trimmed before there was the report of two wherries putting out, signaling they had stores. When informed of this, Commodore Barron wished the wherries, their crews, their captains and their cargoes instant oblivion and told his first officer to keep way on the *Chesapeake,* for he would not bring to now unless commanded by the President himself.

So now the *Chesapeake* gathered speed, wind and tide both serving, and in the British squadron she was watched with professional criticism, for the *Chesapeake* was one of the new Yankee "fir frigates"—the British frigates were of oak. She was not yet ten years old, mounted thirty-six guns, was flush-decked and reckoned faster than anything of her size afloat. She was stiff enough, and although heavy-laden, she slipped through the water without fuss, leaving a clean wake.

Hardly had the *Chesapeake* left, however, when His Majesty's frigate *Leopard* of the British squadron slipped her anchor and stood out after the *Chesapeake.*

"A little trial of speed, I suppose, sir," said Barron's first officer, reporting this. *"Leopard* has the reputation of being fast, particularly off the wind."

"Until we can get this dunnage below, she'll be faster than us on any point of sailing."

Because of the vast amount of deck cargo, the lower sails on the frigate's three masts had not been set, so that she was by no means sailing her fastest. Her hatches were open—they would have to be closed as soon as she cleared the quiet water of the bay and met the ocean rollers—and below decks in the cargo hold a hundred men labored, in dust and gloom, by the light of candle lanterns, moving cargo already stowed to make way for the surplus on the gun decks and main deck.

It wasn't just a matter of making space. The weight of the cargo had to be properly placed or the frigate would sail "crank." The second officer, who was supervising this work, belonged to the old school which insisted that a ship be "trimmed by the stern." By that he meant that the greater weight should be aft of the amidships section. The second officer was a stickler for this kind of stowage and tended toward slowness. So the work of clearing the decks of cargo did not go forward fast. The officer would not allow anything to be brought down from above until all had been made ready for its reception below. He wanted each crate and bale identified as to its contents before it was put in place. Since many of the men in the fog and gloom of below decks were green hands, they became sick and soon useless.

Shortly before noon, *Chesapeake* was off Hampton Roads toward the mouth of the bay and would in fact clear the mouth of the bay in one hour, meeting the ocean rollers driving in before a brisk northeasterly. Her decks were still littered, particularly her main gun deck, which lay below the main deck, where it was difficult to work for lack of room. The gun deck, following the British fashion, was painted dark red, so that blood would not show against its bulwarks to dismay the men when in battle.

*Leopard,* meanwhile, was behaving curiously. She had slipped her anchor some minutes after *Chesapeake* and, crowding on all sail, had followed her down the bay. Despite her spread of canvas, she was not doing well, and the few on *Chesapeake* who had time to spare her a glance concluded that her bottom was foul and she was dragging a garden of barnacles and weeds along with her. However, as the headlands marking the end of the bay came in sight, *Leopard* put on a burst of speed to such good effect that she came within a mile of *Chesapeake.* The officer of the deck on *Chesapeake* kept an eye on her and saw a string of signal flags run up to the forepeak and break loose in the wind.

"*Leopard* is signaling 'Dispatches,' sir," he reported to Barron, who had gone below to his great cabin to be out of sight of that cargo which so annoyed him on his decks.

"Back the foreyards then and heave her to," said Barron. "She has some mail for Europe, no doubt."

This was a courtesy extended between naval vessels of the day—that one would carry dispatches for the other, provided of course their respective nations were not at war. The frigate, which had been running free before a northeasterly, was brought around to the wind, and her foreyards backed so that she hung in the wind's eye, forereaching a little and then falling off.

A boat moved smartly away from the side of the British

frigate, which was also hove to, and had soon reached the side of *Chesapeake*. A lieutenant in a cocked hat, blue coat with gold frogging on the sleeves and pipe-clayed knee breeches swung aboard followed by two seamen. The lieutenant's cutlass hung by a bandoleer across his chest, but the men were not armed. They glanced keenly about at their fellows on the deck of the *Chesapeake*.

"You have dispatches?" asked the *Chesapeake*'s officer.

"A message for your captain."

"I am he," said Barron, who had appeared on deck. "What is it?"

"I am required to present the compliments of Admiral Berkley, commanding His Majesty's ships in these waters, and request the return of several British deserters whom you now have on board your vessel."

"You're *what?*" cried Barron. The message was repeated, while Barron fought to control his temper. To stop an American frigate off her own coast and accuse her of having British deserters aboard was a piece of arrogance the like of which he had not experienced, even in his service against the Tripoli pirates.

"My compliments to Admiral Berkley, Lieutenant," he said. "I have no British deserters aboard my ship. I have three seamen, Americans, who were impressed against their wishes into the King's service, and I have no intention whatever of handing them over to you."

The British lieutenant was not one whit put out. "Admiral Berkley requested that you have the goodness to assemble your ship's company so that I may pick out the men who have deserted from His Majesty's service," he said. "I am familiar with them—in particular with one Jenkin Ratford. The others are known to these two men here." The two English sailors, seeing the American captain so affronted by their officer, were hard put to hide their grins.

"Tell Admiral Berkley to go to perdition," said Captain Barron. "And now, sir, if you will return to your boat, I will get underway."

The lieutenant glanced around the cargo-strewn deck. "Permit me to say that you may have reason to regret this, sir," he said and returned to his boat.

As soon as the boat was clear of the side, *Chesapeake*'s yards were trimmed again and her helm put over to get her underway. Perhaps because of her littered decks, perhaps because her helmsman was busy with the scene which had just taken place before him and so had not his mind on his business, the frigate did not immediately fall off the wind. Indeed, she started to sail backward and her helm had then to be reversed to "box haul" her and get her sailing.

But *Leopard* was having no such trouble. She had been jibbing about during the interview on board the American frigate and a touch of the helm was enough to fill her sails. *Chesapeake*'s officer, with his glass on *Leopard,* saw something happening which astounded him. "She has opened her gunports, sir, and run her guns forward," he cried.

*Leopard* had come downwind on *Chesapeake* and was now no more than three hundred yards off. While the Americans watched in disbelief, there was a thunderous explosion from *Leopard*'s sides, her hull disappeared for a moment in a cloud of snuff-colored smoke, and a second later a broadside flung with a splintering roar into *Chesapeake*'s sides. From somewhere amidships there was a scream, three men staggered backward, and a crimson splash appeared on the side of one of the cargo crates. Captain Barron could not, in that moment, believe that he had been fired upon without warning from a range scarcely more than pistol shot. The crew below, stowing cargo, came pouring out of the main hatch like ants from a nest, thinking that the noise of the broadside was the powder hold exploding.

"Gun stations!" yelled Barron through the speaking trumpet. "Larboard broadside! Lively!"

But the larboard broadside of *Chesapeake*—the only row of guns which could be brought to bear on *Leopard* —was useless. The cargo was cluttering the decks. The guns could not be run up to the gunports. There was no room for the crew to prime and load and swab. The men fought to fling bales and crates and bundles aside to get at the guns, and while they did so, *Leopard,* keeping to windward, wore smartly around and fired again, and again a ton and a half of shot crashed into *Chesapeake*'s unprotected sides.

Two guns had been loaded on *Chesapeake* and run up. *Leopard*'s shot struck one of these and tumbled it off its carriage. The other misfired, through hasty loading, and still the crew tried to clear the gun decks of cargo so they could fight for their ship.

*Leopard* had no intention of giving them such a

38

chance. She crossed the wind once more, fell down on *Chesapeake* again and delivered the full weight of her starboard batteries. The range was so close that *Chesapeake* jerked aside in the water and some of her crew cheered, thinking that it was their own guns that had fired. *Leopard* then drew off in her own smoke and the gunnery officer on *Chesapeake,* trembling with outrage, his face white and distraught, cursed *Leopard,* and cursed the officer in charge of cargo below, and the cargo, and the Navy Department and the whole of the Congress. He dodged along his gun deck, now slippery with blood, for there were many dead and wounded, and finding Barron aft, reported that he could not get a single gun into action, that it was impossible in the state of the ship to even get to the powder hold to bring up more cartridges, and that there were three men dead and a score wounded below so far.

The gunnery officer was so enraged that he came close to giving orders to his own captain. "Lay us alongside," he said. "And I'll take a boarding party over myself and cut down that snot-nosed lieutenant with my own hanger."

Barron was as angry as he but more in control of himself. He had seen action at Tripoli and was not unaccustomed to treachery.

"The guns are useless?" he asked.

"Useless," said the officer.

"Then we must strike our colors and demand an explanation," said Barron.

"Strike?" cried the officer, aghast.

"It will be of little service to our country for me to maintain an attitude of defiance and permit *Leopard* to sink us," said Barron. "We need all the frigates we have. There will be another day, Lieutenant. Pass the word to take down our colors."

The colors, flying at the peak of the mizzen gaff, were lowered, and the frigate once more turned into the wind and her foreyards backed. The same lieutenant who had first boarded *Chesapeake* returned and climbed aboard again. He glanced at the lowered ensign and said, "Admiral Berkley's compliments and will you kindly muster your crew for inspection so that known deserters from His Britannic Majesty's vessels can be taken off."

"What you are doing is an act of piracy, abhorrent to the civilized world," said Barron. "You have fired on a helpless vessel three times, killed several of her crew, wounded a score of others, and now demand license to remove men whom you call deserters. You disgrace your flag, sir, and you disgrace the King under whom you serve and the nation to which you belong."

"If you will have the goodness to give the order for the mustering of all your hands, I will do my duty," said the lieutenant. A faint pink flush showed, however, that Barron's words had not left him unmoved. He hesitated and added. "I feel I must answer the charge of firing on a helpless vessel. Your broadside is of more weight than the *Leopard*'s, sir. You are a ship of war, and by no means helpless."

"You can see for yourself that my guns cannot be served," replied Barron.

"That is a matter of ship management for which you can hardly hold His Britannic Majesty or his officers responsible," said the lieutenant.

"I would remind you that our nations are at peace and you have fired on this vessel," said Barron.

"The mustering of the hands, sir, if you please," said the lieutenant. "Perhaps your bosun will call them?"

Captain Barron gave the order, turned on his heel and walked off to his cabin. The hands were lined up on the deck among the cargo and the lieutenant went through them, staring into each man's face. He found himself opposite the *Chesapeake*'s bosun and smiled. "Well, Ratford," he said. "You didn't know how valuable a man you were when you deserted, did you? Worth three broadsides, several men dead and, I should think, three-score lashes with the cat. There'll just be enough of you left, Ratford, when we're through with you, to answer to your name and nothing more."

Ratford, his eyes wild, darted for the side but was seized by the two British seamen and flung into the bottom of their boat, his hands and feet bound. From there he hailed the *Chesapeake*. "Goodbye, mates," he said. "This is the last you'll ever see of me." One of the seamen in the boat silenced him by a blow on the head with a bailing bucket. Three other men were taken from *Chesapeake,* all of whom claimed that they were Americans.

"So much the worse for you," said the lieutenant, leaving the ship. "Americans are nothing but British rebels. A strange defense, indeed—not guilty by virtue of rebellion." He gave a sharp thin supercilious laugh and told the coxon to cast off.

On *Chesapeake* the smoldering crew turned to tend to their wounded and their dead.

# 5

*F*ᴏʀ the next week Manly Treegate heard nothing but talk of the attack on the *Chesapeake* and of the imminent war with England. Business in Norfolk seemed to cease entirely, and wherever he went with his uncle (and he went to a great number of remarkable places), the conversation invariably started with the attack and ended with the attack, the business of the moment being tucked in wherever room could be found for it.

Everybody believed that the President would now ask the Congress for a declaration of war, as required under the Constitution, and the Congress would, without debate, pass that declaration—everybody believed this except Peter Treegate. His view was that the President would not go to war with Great Britain. There would be no war despite the fact that a British frigate had, without provocation, opened fire on an American frigate and in American waters.

"The French are the true wolves in any case," he said. "The British fight for survival. France has conquered the greater part of Europe and Napoleon will not rest until he has it all. We in America, exporting and importing goods, will have to dance to a French fiddler and would be dancing to one now, perhaps, if it were not for Britain."

"Are you forgetting that France sold us the whole of the Louisiana Territory and at a most reasonable price?" said the warehouse manager with whom this conversation took place.

"Because, if she did not sell it to us, she would lose it to the British fleet," said Peter Treegate. "The French Navy does not amount to a tattered coast guard since Trafalgar and could never have held New Orleans against a British attack."

"Mr. Treegate," said the other with some heat, "do you *dare* to take the part of that nation which wantonly attacked our ship and from which we have but recently— in your lifetime and mine—wrested our freedom?"

"I take the part of the United States of America," said Peter Treegate. "War with Britain now would seal up all our ports, cripple our export and import trade, destroy our economy, and gain us nothing. The people may ring the bells for war now. But they would wring their hands because of it in a year or two."

"And the *Chesapeake,* sir," said the other. "What of that? Are we to allow this insult to our flag?"

"When a bully beats a helplesss man, who is shamed —the bully or the victim?" asked Peter Treegate. "Again, if *Chesapeake* could not reply to *Leopard,* how do you think our little fleet of frigates and sloops of war is to reply to the might of the British Navy? Or is it your opinion that the outcome of a war does not matter, so long as the war is fought?"

Many such conversations left Manly Treegate first confused and then bored. The matter was quite clear in his own mind. An American ship had been attacked. The Americans ought to attack the British squadron still lying in the Chesapeake—or at least help the French to attack them.

Many in Norfolk—indeed, the whole city, it seemed— were of the same opinion. When *Chesapeake* came back to put her dead and wounded ashore and report on the whole matter, Norfolk erupted with anger against the British, and a dozen schemes for revenge were proposed, including an offer by a committee of seamen to man the French vessels if they would attack the British squadron. All shore leave from the British ships was stopped immediately and all intercourse with the shore cut off. The British put picket boats about their ships to prevent their anchor hawsers being cut during the night by irate Americans. Even with the picket boats out, scores of bumboats, small barges, long boats and other craft went out so their passengers could shout abuse and defiance at the British ships, and the men on the waterfront did a brisk business, at a shilling a head, providing patriotic citizens with a chance to get near the British ships and shout their insults and warnings at their grim black-and-white sides.

A day or two later Manly Treegate had a chance to do the same. His uncle was going for the afternoon to an estate up the James River, and the boy begged to be allowed to stay in Norfolk and explore the place and countryside around alone.

"All right," said Peter Treegate. "I may be away over-night, but you are to be here at Sutro's Hotel at sundown tomorrow. Here is five shillings. If you hire a horse, see that you pay no more than sixpence for a well-groomed animal and take a look at the shoes. If you bring the horse back lame, they will charge you for the shoeing, and there is more money made that way than by actual hire."

"Yes, sir," said Manly.

"You will perhaps bathe in the bay. Can you swim?"

"A little, sir," said Manly.

"That is something I never learned," said Peter Treegate. "Well, be back at sundown. Do nothing foolish." So they parted, and Manly Treegate, thrilled at being entirely alone and with five shillings in his pocket, decided that he would hire a horse, the better to explore the whole place.

There was a livery stable close to Sutro's Hotel, a large one, providing both riding and carriage horses, and here Manly asked for a mount and was brought a large grey plug with a cast in one eye.

"That won't do," he told the hostler. "Bring me a better mount than that."

"What do you know about 'orses?" said the hostler. "You'd better take what's offered, young gentleman, or you'll get worse, or none at all."

46

For answer Manly put a penny in the hostler's hand and went down through the stalls himself. He came on a big black mount he liked, but it shied as he passed by, so he knew it was no horse for riding. He passed up a nice chestnut mare and hesitated over a paint gelding, finally settling for a small white horse, broad-chested and with a black blaze on its forehead.

"Good for twenty miles at a hard gallop," said the hostler approvingly. "You'll be from one of the plantations upriver, no doubt."

"No," said Manly. "I'm from Salem, Massachusetts."

"Going for a trot along the bay?" asked the hostler, flinging a saddle over the horse. Manly nodded.

"Might stop at the Three Jolly Pigeons, about three miles down," said the hostler. "Famous place in these parts. Rest the horse. Get a bite and a sup."

"What's it famous for?" asked Manly.

"Why, Nollichucky Jack was there many a time. Him and Treegate of Treegate's Raiders. In and out they was, and the country thick with Redcoats. That Frenchman was there too. Lafeet, I think his name was."

"Lafayette," said Manly, thrilled to discover how famous his uncle was. He was strongly tempted to announce his identity but didn't.

"No. Lafeet or something," said the hostler. "They say he's got a son that's a kind of a pirate down there in New Orleans. Lafeet. That's it. Foreign name. Frenchman. There's some of 'em good and some of 'em bad, but they're all foreigners. Don't ever forget that."

The horse was now saddled and the boy mounted

readily, without the aid of the mounting block, and once in the saddle gave a sixpence to the hostler.

"And what might your name be, young sir?" asked the hostler.

"Treegate," said the boy, and without waiting for his reaction, he led the horse out into the sunlight and down the street. The hostler squinted after him for a while and then spat with enormous deliberation into the straw at his feet.

"There's getting to be more liars in the world with every generation that's born," he said. "Things go on like this, my grandchildren ain't going to hear the truth spoken all their lives."

Manly had explored the docks sufficiently with his uncle, so he turned away from them and was soon riding down dusty, tree-lined streets, the trees throwing great splotches of cool shade on the red dust. In a little while he was on a well-kept road, headed south through rolling countryside with tilled fields on either hand. There were great flocks of birds about—starlings and waxwings and even gulls wheeling in from the bay. Manly passed a heavy coach lumbering up a hill, with the outside passengers walking in the swirling dust and the coachman's dog padding along between the axles in the shade.

Riding was a great delight. The stout little mare cantered happily along, with a stride that just suited the boy, though it would have been uncomfortable for a man. Manly waved his hat as he passed the lumbering coach, and the passengers grinned or glowered at him according to their dispositions. He topped the hill and reined in to take in the view. Like waves of the sea, but green rather than blue, the fields flowed from him in every direction to the horizon. Far away, a flashing splinter of light marked the mouth of the great bay, the Chesapeake. To his left, some miles distant, the arm of the bay stretched from north to south, now hidden behind hills, now showing in stretches of glassy green.

Here and there among the billows of the hills was a white-painted farm or estate house, usually in its own copse of trees, planted to provide summer shade and winter shelter. The hill on which he reined in his mare was not very high. Yet it commanded a tremendous view over the low but rolling delta country, and Manly, who had never thought of these things, reflected on what a rich and comfortable and safe country it was—the land tilled and neat, the fields fenced, the roads well laid out and the houses decently painted and in excellent repair.

Following along the line of the road, he saw that it came to a rather larger house, which seemed to be located right beside the bay. He decided that that must be the Three Jolly Pigeons Inn of which the hostler had told him, and he decided too that it would be an excellent place to eat something and give the mare a bite and a drop of water too, though he would not give her much with a long ride still ahead of him.

Off he went down the road, the wind hissing past his ears and his long hair trailing out behind him under his hat, for the ribbon with which it was tied had come loose and he had no inclination to stop and retie it.

The mare was a sturdy little creature and he had soon

reached the inn and dismounted. The mare was sweating a bit from her exertion, but would take no harm for the day was warm. Manly asked for some bread and cheese and cider, which cost him five pence, and settled with these on a bench outside the inn, listening to the drone of the bees in the gardens nearby and watching the dappling of the shadows thrown on the road before him by a huge oak.

Scarcely two hundred yards away was the bay, with a little jetty running out into it, and tied to the jetty a small catboat, her sail furled along the long boom. The bread had a good thick crust, the cheese was sharp and the cider had a sweet bite to it, and all these pleasures suggested somehow one more pleasure which was this—why not make the fullest use of this day of freedom by going for a sail on the bay?

Manly was a good sailor. He had lived in Boston before his father died and they had spent many hours sailing together on the bay and on the lower reaches of the Charles River. He eyed the catboat and glanced at the sun. It was not yet noon, he decided. He could spend a couple of hours sailing in the bay, maybe go for a swim, and still be in plenty of time to get back to Sutro's Hotel by six as he had promised.

He brushed the crumbs of bread and cheese off his lap and sauntered down to the jetty to look the boat over. She was bluff-bowed, clinker-built, and bigger than he had thought, for she was about twenty feet long with a beam of half that amount. She had a big centerboard and two curious winches, one on each side, which Manly decided were used for hauling in a net. She was used perhaps for dredging oysters, but, this not being the oyster season, was idle now.

While he was looking at her, a man appeared, walking along the jetty toward him. He had a tarpot in one hand and a brush made of teased-out rope strands in the other. He walked past Manly and got into the boat, dumping the tarpot in the bilges with no great grace. Then he sat down on the stern sheets and looked up at Manly on the jetty. "If you are looking for a sail, the answer is no," he said. "This boat ain't for hire for under a shilling."

To this surprising announcement Manly said nothing. The man searched in the pocket of his ragged canvas pants and took out a dirty piece of string, a jackknife, a piece of beeswax, a sailmaker's palm, a small wood box containing fishhooks, and eventually a plug of tobacco. There were some threads and some crumbs of moldy bread stuck to the tobacco and he rubbed them off with a horny thumbnail and took a bite off the plug. Then he returned all his belongings to his pocket.

"Got to tar her bilges," he said, one thin yellow cheek enormously distended by the lump of tobacco in it. "Got to tar her bilges and here's Sue Anne screaming her head off and the thirteen children all running around the house except Sarah that's sick with croup and young Ted-John that's helping with the hoeing. And them four Leghorns ain't laid one egg all week, tarnation take 'em. Did you ever hear that Leghorns won't lay if they gets into cotton seed?"

"No," said Manly, "but I don't know much about hens."

"Me neither," said the man. "But don't never buy

Leghorns. They're more trouble than a topmast scow in a northeast gale. Four of 'em, mind you, scratching and pecking and squawking around all week and not an egg among 'em." He ejected a stream of tobacco juice into the tarpot and then, by way of excusing himself, said, "Keep's them marine borers and barnacles down. Helps thin it out, too."

"Supposing I offered you a shilling to hire the boat," said Manly. "Wouldn't that make up for no eggs?"

"No," said the man. "On account of you ain't got a shilling."

"Oh yes, I have," said Manly and produced one.

The man looked at it and shook his head solemnly. "That's what tears your heart out," he said. "Here's me with Sue Anne screeching and thirteen children screaming about the place and four Leghorns that won't lay nohow, and me days filled with work and no profit from it, and there's you, just a boy, with no wife and no children and no work and your pocket filled with money. I won't say one word against the Lord that made me, but I'll say this—He don't know the half of what's going on in the world."

"You can have the shilling if you'll rent me the boat," said Manly. "Three hours. There'll still be time to tar her bilges."

"And me have to go back to Sue Anne and all them screaming children?" said the other.

"All right. You can come with me," said Manly. "But in that case I will only pay you eightpence."

"You from these parts?" asked the man.

"No. I'm not."

"Well, I'm glad of that," said the other, "because the kind of bargain you drive, you'd own the whole of Virginia by the time you're twenty. Eightpence it is. Get aboard and lively before Sue Anne comes to see how I'm getting along with the tarring."

# 6

*T*HE man's name was Coffin, Manly learned—Tobias Coffin. He was tall, narrow-shouldered and his skin had a greyish tinge to it, as if some of the fine grey mud from the bilges of his boat had worked its way into his pores and could not be removed. He talked about his troubles all the time, and his life seemed to be but a prolonged cause for complaint and he the victim of every circumstance.

He was a good sailor, however. While Manly let the centerboard down and stepped the tiller in its gudgeons, Coffin loosened the sail, raising it on the stumpy mast and belaying the halyard forward in the bow, where it served the additional purpose of a forestay. Manly then went forward to push the boat's head off while Coffin took the tiller, and in a moment the sail had filled and they were moving fast out into the waters of the bay. Coffin handled

54

the tiller lightly, luffing up with every freshening of the wind and then falling off a little when the air went light, so that he kept the oyster boat moving fast, throwing a bubbling wake in the green water behind her.

"There's two of President Thomas Jefferson's gunboats," he said as they slid past two bargelike vessels swinging on moorings. Each mounted two twenty-pounders—one up forward and one aft by the steersman. They were both sloop-rigged. "Now what's the use of them things?" asked Coffin. "No use at all. Beats me how a man can be President and a born fool as well. Why, anybody can see with half an eye that they'd founder in a moderate sea. And who would want to take one of them things, with but two guns on it, out against a thirty-six-gun frigate?" Manly looked the gunboats over carefully. His uncle had told him that Mr. Jefferson put enormous faith in them as protection for the nation's seaports. They seemed clumsy to him, but he replied that twenty or thirty of them, not one, would be a match for a frigate or something even bigger.

"No, they wouldn't," said Coffin. "They ain't a match for nothing and I'll tell you why. First, they can't take any kind of a sea; they founder, for the guns makes them top-heavy. Second, they're so low in the water, their shot goes under the sea instead of lofting for a while through the air. Third, a frigate can fire all her guns on one side at once—say eighteen guns to a broadside. But you can't even expect twenty gunboats to fire together—not unless you want to put them all on land, and what good are boats on land? I tell you, this country is in a poor way when we got a President who is as big a fool as Tom Jefferson. And if ever I was to see him, I'd tell him so myself plain."

"Let me take the tiller now," said Manly.

"You sure you can handle her?" asked Coffin.

"Yes."

"Well, watch the end of that boom. It's long and low and if it touched a wave she'll breach and we'll both be in for a swim." Manly nodded and took the tiller. He was surprised at how readily the boat answered, and tightening the sheet, he came closer to the wind in order to move northward up the bay. This course also took them farther away from the land. After a while they could make out one lone, three-masted vessel at anchor in the middle of the roadstead, something like two miles from the nearest point of land.

"You think that Mr. Jefferson's gunboats are a match for her?" asked Coffin.

"Who is she?" asked Manly.

"Why, that's the frigate *Leopard* that fired on *Chesapeake* so that we will be at war pretty soon, and I don't know how many thousands of people killed and towns burned to the ground and children left homeless and cattle and horses driven off or let loose on the roads and fields, not to speak of hens. And all because Tom Jefferson is such a fool."

"I don't think Mr. Jefferson had anything to do with *Chesapeake* being fired on," said Tom.

"Well, if you ain't as big a fool as he is," said Coffin. "Isn't he President? If we had eight three-deckers in Chesapeake Bay instead of one frigate and them silly gunboats, nobody would never have fired on *Chesapeake*. Better head her a little east. Don't go near that frigate. She's got picket boats out, thinking people will cut her hawser or set her afire, which they ought by rights do."

"We can go a little closer," said Manly. "I want to get a look at her guns."

The frigate *Leopard* was still two miles off, so Coffin was plainly being overcautious. Manly ignored him. He headed the little catboat directly for the frigate, and with the wind now stiffer since they were approaching the middle of the bay, she sped along, making a little wash under her lee, and Manly could feel the tiller trembling in his hand, such was her speed. Soon the frigate was much nearer and the picket boats no more than a quarter of a mile off. The picket boats, however, seemed to be busy with a problem of their own. There were three of them, and a lot of hailing was going on back and forth. They came together and there was a consultation among the officers in charge. Then they separated and, forming a line abreast, started moving down the bay, the steersmen standing up and looking about them as they went.

"They're looking for something," said Manly.

"Boat exercises," said Coffin. "We're getting too near that danged frigate. I don't like to be that close. We should steer off."

"She can do us no harm," said Manly. "Can you make out whether her gunports are open?"

"You'll never see the guns," said Coffin. "They're run back in their breechings. Head her off now. You're too close. There'll be trouble if you don't."

A voice now hailed them from the bulwarks of the

frigate, telling them to stand clear. Manly felt a surge of irritation at being ordered about by a British ship in American waters and did not move the helm immediately. Then a marine on the spar deck of the frigate raised his musket and there was a report, and a long plume of smoke jutted from the weapon. That was too much for Coffin. He took the tiller, put it hard over, and the catboat flung across the wind and darted away from the frigate toward the shore.

"They've no right to fire on us," said Manly.

"They didn't have no right to fire on *Chesapeake* either," said Coffin. "We might have been killed, both of us, because of you. If that marine had just taken it into his head to aim, I could be floating down the bay now. I could be dead as a mackerel, with the blood all streaming from me, and Sue Anne wouldn't never see me again. Dead as a mackerel and blood floating all over the bay." He seemed to find pleasure in the prospect.

"It was only a warning shot," said Manly.

"Maybe my body wouldn't never be found," said Coffin. "Just float on out to sea to be eaten by the fish, and people would wonder for years whatever became of me."

"If you were shot by a British marine, the whole of Norfolk would know about it," said Manly.

This pleased Coffin greatly. "There'd be speeches given and music played," Coffin said. "They'd say that I died a noble defender of the freedom of the Sons of Liberty." Manly was only half listening. Ahead, silhouetted against the westering sun, was a channel marker. It consisted of a large barrel tarred black—perhaps warning of a shoal extending out from the Virginia coast. There were many such markers on the bay: some painted red, meaning that they were not to be passed on the portside going down the bay; and some black, which meant that they were not to be passed to larboard. What interested Manly about this marker, however, was that there was a large seal trying to get onto it but failing every time as the barrel turned in the water.

He pointed the marker out to Coffin, who was still rehearsing his own funeral, and Coffin squinted his eyes against the dancing glitter of the sun on the water and said, "That ain't no seal. That's a man. That's what that is." He pulled the helm up, tacking the boat so as to stay away from the buoy. "We'd best steer clear of him," he said.

"You can't leave him there in the middle of the bay," cried Manly. "He'll drown."

"So he likely will," said Coffin. "Unless them picket boats pick him up. But that ain't none of our business. He's a deserter. That's what he is. And he is as good as dead anyway, because he will either drown or if they find him, why, they'll flog him to death."

"He's waving to us," said Manly. "We can't leave him there."

"Yes, we can," said Coffin. "And that's what we're going to do. Because you know what happened to *Chesapeake* when she had deserters on board, and knowing that, you can judge what would happen to us. Dead. With a musket ball through our breasts, and blood pouring all over the bay."

Manly glanced around. The distance from the ship to

the buoy was close to two miles. The picket boats were a mile to the south of them and headed away. "We could pick him up without anybody seeing us," said Manly. "It would be easy."

"Don't suppose he's got as much as a penny on him," said Coffin. "It's risky. Unmercifully risky. And I got thirteen children to feed and not a morsel of help from them hens, as I was telling you earlier." He gave Manly a calculating look. "Now, supposing we was to just make a board in that direction and then we was to just happen to come about right off the buoy—say, about four feet from it, which ain't no distance for a seaman—and he was to let go of it and come tumbling over our gunwale. That ought to be worth a shilling if it was properly handled."

"Certainly," said Manly. "I'll give you a shilling and gladly."

"Well, then, stand to the sheet," said Coffin. "And watch that boom when she tacks. It settles down a bit and the sea is rising with the tide coming up the bay. So bring it in handily." Manly did as bid, and the catboat was put about on the other tack and now sped once more toward the buoy. The man, seeing them coming, raised an arm, and at the same time Coffin, his eye on the brig, called out that she was signaling her boats. Manly looked quickly about and saw that the lead boat had turned in their direction and was hoisting a lugsail.

"They've seen him too," he cried. "But we are much nearer. We can pick him up and make the shore with him, and they won't dare land."

The buoy was now only fifty yards off, and the seaman

clinging to it let go and started to splash his way toward them. He was a very poor swimmer but willing to risk anything to make his escape. He got to the side of the catboat, and Coffin reached over and grabbed him under an arm and got him halfway in. The man was too weak or too clumsy to help himself, and he lay half in the boat and half in the water, while Coffin struggled with him, neglecting the tiller for a moment. The boat fell off the wind, very nearly driving the seaman under, for he was now under the lee. Coffin gave a tremendous heave to get him aboard, and at that moment the sail filled, the boom struck the water and the foot of the sail was buried in it.

For a moment the catboat hung on the edge of capsizing. Then, without a sound, it tipped over and the three of them were floundering in the water, tangled in the sail and the mainsheet and with no hope whatever of getting the boat back on its keel in a hurry.

The picket boat came up in a moment and the unfortunate seaman, offering no resistance, was hauled aboard. The lieutenant in charge grinned at Manly and Coffin clinging to the side of their overturned boat. "Three birds with one stone," he said. "That's a fair return for a little effort. All right, on board with you."

"Not I," cried Coffin. "I'm a citizen of the United States of America and you can't take me." A moment later he was looking down the barrel of a formidable-looking musket wielded by the sole marine in the picket boat. Coffin, without a further word, climbed into the picket boat. There was nothing Manly could do to resist. He thought for a moment of striking out for the shore, but the distance was too great. Strong hands seized him and he was hauled into the picket boat.

The lieutenant eyed the catboat and then told two of his men to go over the side, bail her, right her, and bring her back to the frigate. She could fetch five pounds at an auction and that would be five pounds for the lieutenant's pocket.

"I don't know when I'm ever going to see Sue Anne again," said Coffin, climbing up the sides. "I should have done what she said to do and tarred the bilges of that there boat."

# 7

WHEN they were aboard the frigate, Manly and Coffin were left standing by one of the guns for some time, guarded by a marine. Then there was the shrilling of a bosun's pipe, the piercing sound rising and falling in a ridiculous manner as if to parody melody, and this was followed by a tremendous scuttering of bare feet. Soon the deck of the frigate was filled with men, some of whom had to climb into the lower shrouds and up on the gunwale to find footing. The petty officers of the crew—bosuns, coxons, carpenters and others—were in front of this multitude and the rest behind, all of them facing aft to the quarterdeck, which was at the moment occupied by first and second lieutenants and the sailing master. When all had gathered there, the captain appeared—a brisk, fierce, small man, with a face as brown as snuff and furrowed, it seemed, by the winds and waves of all the seas of the world. He had clapped a cocked hat on his head, pulled down over his eyes, so that in the sunlight only the tip of his nose and the point of his chin were illuminated. Up to the moment when the captain appeared, there had been a slight rustling and jostling among the men, but as soon as he was in sight, this was entirely gone. A silence, rigid as marble, descended over the whole crew.

The captain came to the short rail which separated the quarterdeck from the main deck below, and with his hands behind his back he stared at his crew. Satisfied with this survey, he addressed them in a voice so soft it was only with difficulty that Manly could hear what he said.

"Lieutenant Bowers tells me that he has captured a deserter and also two civilians who had entered into a conspiracy to aid his desertion," he said. "That conspiracy consisted of a plan whereby the deserter would swim to a channel buoy and wait there until the conspirators came by in a boat from the shore to pick him up."

"That's not true," cried Manly.

All eyes turned to him.

"If you do not maintain silence," said the captain gently, "I will have to see that silence is imposed upon you. I would advise you to remain quiet until you are given permission to speak." The marine guard beside him, without moving a muscle of his face or changing the direction of his stare, which was toward the captain and the quarterdeck, said, "Shut up, young 'un, if you want to keep your teeth."

All heads returned to the quarterdeck and the captain said to Lieutenant Bowers, "Read the penalty for desertion." Bowers opened a book he was carrying and, looking at the captain, without even a glance at the open page, he said, "Desertion in time of war shall be punishable by death by hanging, or by such lesser penalty as the captain at his discretion may impose. Desertion in sight of the enemy shall be punishable by death by hanging with no discretion allowed to the captain."

"In sight of the enemy," said the captain. "An important point, that. Were we in sight of the French at the time this man left his ship?"

"No, sir," said the lieutenant, and Manly got the impression that the question and the reply had been rehearsed. "No French vessel was in sight at that time."

"A singularly fortunate circumstance for the prisoner," said the captain. "Bring him here."

The man had been kept to one side under a guard of marines. He was now brought forward, shivering, still wet, his figure bowed and his eyes staring at the deck.

"Since you were taken red-handed, I assume you have no defense to offer," said the captain. "However, do you have anything at all to say before I decide your punishment?" The man mumbled something which was quite inaudible and was told to speak up by Lieutenant Bowers. The captain still could not hear what the man said, and one of the marines asked permission to speak for him.

"Go ahead," said the captain.

"He says there was no conspiracy, sir," said the marine. "The boat come on him by chance."

"I shall be the judge of that," said the captain.

"He says if it's flogging, he'd sooner be hung."

"Very sensible, too," said the captain. "However, it will

65

be a rare day when a prisoner can pick his own punishment.

"Forty lashes," said the captain. "All hands to witness
punishment. The petty officers will report to me anyone
who turns his head away or closes his eyes, and such a
man can expect to receive a taste of that at which he could
not look. Surgeon, you will examine the man after every
five blows and see whether he is capable of withstanding
more.

"And now bring these other two before me while the
prisoner is tied up."

Coffin and Manly were now brought to the front while
the deserter's wrists were tied to the main shrouds in such
a position that he could not rest on the flat of his feet but
was hung up by his wrists.

"Read the charge," said the captain. "You are charged
with conspiring to aid and aiding a seaman of His
Britannic Majesty's Navy to desert his duty and his ship in
time of war," said Lieutenant Bowers. "The witness
against you are the crew of three picket boats, their
officers and myself."

What followed was no trial at all. Perhaps if Coffin had
not got involved in explanations about Sue Anne and his
children and his hens and how he was going to tar his
boat, they would have done better. But he *did* get involved and the captain's patience was exhausted in a very
short time. Manly insisted that he was visiting Norfolk
from Salem, that he knew nobody in the area and that he
was with his uncle, Peter Treegate, who had given him
money and a free day while he himself visited some
friends in the interior. For one golden moment Manly

thought that he at least might be let free. But the lieutenant whispered something to the captain, and whatever it was, the decision went against him.

"It is quite plain to me," said the captain, "that whether you actually conspired with this man to desert or not, you certainly intended to help him. You took him off the buoy and into your own boat, and by thus aiding in the flight of a seaman from one of His Britannic Majesty's ships, you have utterly lost your position as a neutral and civilian and are entitled to no protection whatever from your own government."

He turned to the lieutenant and said very casually, "Get their names and enter them on the ship's roll. They must witness punishment with the rest."

Manly never forgot the horror of the punishment. The man let out one scream as the first blow fell, and thereafter he was incapable of getting enough breath to cry out. The deck around became splattered with blood, which fell on those who were closest. But the full forty lashes were not administered, for after the first ten the surgeon, who was also the ship's carpenter, reported that the man was dying and could take no more. He was dead the following morning and his body sewn in an old sail, and he was put over the side after a perfunctory service which the whole crew was assembled to witness, as they had been previously assembled to see the man flogged to death.

Peter Treegate returned from his visit to the county behind Norfolk at noon on the following day. He was disturbed to find that Manly had not returned to Sutro's

Hotel and started an immediate hunt for him. The hostler in the livery stable provided the first clue to the boy's whereabouts, saying that he had hired a white mare and gone riding. "Don't understand why he ain't back though," the hostler said. "He knew how to ride. That's for sure. So he wouldn't have been thrown. Tarnation liar, though. Said his name was Treegate, same as the man organized the raiders during the rebellion."

"Did the boy say where he was going?" asked Mr. Treegate.

"No, sir, he didn't," said the man. "Wait a minute, now. He was talking about the Three Jolly Pigeons and I'll stake my best rig that's where he went."

There was a horse, a big hunter, saddled nearby, awaiting the arrival of another of the hotel guests. Peter Treegate, without a word to the hostler, leaped into the saddle and set off down the road at a gallop, leaving the hostler staring after him openmouthed.

Manly's white mare was still at the stable of the Three Jolly Pigeons. But nobody knew where Manly had gone. The tapman said he had heard of somebody drowned down the bay when a boat overturned, and one of the waiters said he'd heard of a lost boy ten miles down the road at a place called Saltpool, but he was reminded that that was four weeks ago. Several of the people at the inn remembered Manly sitting outside eating his bread and cheese and drinking his cider. But nobody could recall seeing him leave.

"Might have been kidnapped," said the stableman. "This is a post road and there's all kinds of people going along it."

"Did you see him talking to anybody?" Mr. Treegate asked, but nobody had. Then the tapman spoke to the cellarman, who was bringing up a new butt of claret ("You should try a glass, sir. 'Ninety-two and we won't see any more like it, the way that war's dragging on"), and the cellarman remarked that there were a lot of people disappearing from the neighborhood and, if anybody asked him, he'd say it was the tarnation British fleet hanging around Hampton Roads that was responsible.

"Tobias Coffin's gone too," he said. "Him that had the little oyster boat down the end of the jetty. Went down there yesterday, his wife told me, to tar the bilges, and she hasn't seen neither him nor the boat since. It's the Britishers, without any doubt," he continued. "They say them ships is so undermanned from desertions and war losses that they can't fight them and can hardly sail them. And they're so hungry for men, they'd take the Lord Mayor at his banquet, and all the guests too, if there wasn't a guard of militia put around them."

Mr. Treegate found Mrs. Coffin in a confusion of children and hens, and confirmed that her husband and his boat were missing.

"Perhaps he is out fishing," he suggested.

"Not this time of the year, sir," she said.

"If the boat's gone, it is likely that my nephew persuaded him to take him for a sail," said Mr. Treegate. "Is there another boat to be had?"

"What good would it do to go searching the bay for them now?" asked Mrs. Coffin. "That's a mighty big bay. If they were swamped, that happened a long time ago and they'd either be ashore now or drowned. Best search along the shore, sir, and see if they had to put in at some distant place."

Since there was nothing more to be gained at the Three Jolly Pigeons, Mr. Treegate set out on the hunter along the margin of the bay, having first paid the stableman to saddle a horse and search the shore in the other direction. Enough stir was now made about the missing boy for any who heard any rumors about him to report to the Three Jolly Pigeons. Mr. Treegate struck southward then, and three miles or so away, coming to a little stream, he saw beside it a boathouse and an old man sitting in the sun smoking his pipe. Here he inquired for Manly or any news of a boat which might have capsized on the bay.

"Well, now," said the old man, "I did see a catboat out on the bay about this time yesterday afternoon. And although it was three miles away, I could see there was two folk in it. And I think I know where they are now."

"Where?" demanded Mr. Treegate.

"On that there frigate," said the old man, pointing with his pipe. "They was swamped. And the picket boats to that frigate took them up, or so it seemed to me, though it is hard to tell at that distance. Anyway, when they was swamped, I saw the picket boats close in on them and then tow their boat over to the frigate. That I saw plain."

"Do you have a boat you can let me have?" asked Mr. Treegate.

"I do," said the old man. "But if you're thinking of going out to that frigate, it won't do you no use. She's picking up her anchor now."

It was true. The frigate's topsails flashed white in the

sun, and as more and more sail was piled on her masts, she started to move down the bay.

"I must stop her," cried Mr. Treegate. "If what you say is true, my nephew is on board. It is he who was out in the catboat with the other man."

The old man knocked the ashes out of his pipe in the palm of his withered hand.

"There isn't nothing you can do for him, sir," he said. "There'll be maybe a score of Americans in that ship at this moment. Dutchmen, too. And French. And enough blacks to run a plantation. And nothing anybody can do. It's a hard thing to say, but should your nephew be aboard that frigate, you will likely never see him again."

# 8

DURING the first few hours of captivity, Manly clung to the hope that his uncle would find him and release him. That hope faded to all but nothing when the frigate sailed from the Chesapeake. He knew then he would not see his uncle again for years, if at all, and burst into tears.

Manly had been confined, while the frigate was at anchor, in the cockpit of the vessel, deep down in one of her aft holds, to prevent his escape. There was no porthole to look out of and no more air or light than could seep in from an open hatch ten feet overhead. There was no way out of the cockpit, for the ladder which he was forced to descend to enter it had been withdrawn. He was left there alone through the night and the following morning. He had not even the company of Coffin, who was taken elsewhere. He was given nothing either to eat or to drink, and he spent the time overwhelmed by the terrible change in his fortunes and sick with horror at the flogging of the seaman.

Only when the frigate was underway was he allowed out of the hold. He was handed over to a bosun's mate called Steever, who told him he was to berth with the crew of number-six gun, portside.

"Could I have something to eat?" asked Manly.

"You'll mess with your gun crew at sundown," said Steever. "Off with you."

It was not easy to find his gun crew. There was more shadow than light on the gun deck, which was below the spar deck. The place was a terrible confusion of coiled ropes, buckets, rammers, shot, shot racks, cartridge racks and stowed hammocks, with as many as two hundred men busy at a bewildering variety of duties—among them the closing of the gunports, since the frigate would soon be in the ocean. As each gunport was closed and secured, there was less and less light. At last Manly found a boy of his own age, rather better dressed than the gunners, and asked him where he could find number-six gun, portside.

"Damn your eyes, say 'sir' when you talk to a ship's officer," said the boy. He struck Manly full in the face, hard enough to knock him to the deck. Before he could get up, a seaman had pinned him to the deck, kneeling across him.

"Lie still," he said. "That's a midshipman." Then turning to the midshipman, he said, "Green hand, sir, begging your pardon. I'll take care of him."

"See he learns ship's ways," said the boy and passed on

disdainfully, the gunners and seamen being very careful to move aside for him.

"Young 'un," said the man who had prevented Manly retaliating, "no matter who hits you, shoves you, spits at you or tries to kill you on board this here ship, don't do nothing back. Because if you do, you'll be flogged, and your age won't save you. I seen boys of seven flogged here until they couldn't remember their own names. So watch yourself. What gun are you assigned to?"

Manly told him.

"That's mine," said the man. "And this here's the gun. Get over there among the hammocks to be out of harm's way."

The seamen's hammocks were lashed against the bulwark to the side of the gun, where in action they would serve to prevent splinters flying about the gun deck. They formed a thick padding of canvas against which Manly squatted while the shot was secured in the racks, the gun lashed to iron rings in the deck and wedges driven under the wheels of the gun carriage so they could not move with the rolling of the frigate.

When this was done, a bosun's mate inspected the work, and he being satisfied, the gunport of that particular gun was closed. Once it was closed and fastened firmly shut, a little slit of brilliant light from the sides and bottom of the gunport sliced across the gloom of the gun deck, and the faces and figures of the gunners, caught for a moment in this as they passed to and fro, became grotesque, as if they were so many demons inhabiting a pit.

Soon all the guns were secured and the ports closed,

and the whole gun deck became a series of narrow panels of light thrusting in through the sides and bottoms of the gunports. No attempt was made to caulk these, for the gun deck was fitted with scuppers, so whatever water came in through the gunports went out through the scuppers. But a canvas bag was put over the breech of the gun to prevent spray wetting the touchhole, and the muzzle was fitted with a stopper called a tampion.

Number-six gun, portside, Manly found, was actually the seventh from the bow. It was called number six because it had once been six, and whatever anything was once, it remained to the end of its days in the Royal Navy. The gunner who had befriended Manly said his name was Weeks.

"You'll get used to the life," he said. "If you don't think about your life before, and you don't go thinking about what's to come either but just keep your mind on what's happening right now, it ain't that bad. And there's always a chance of action," he added with a touch of pleasure.

Almost all the men on the frigate, Manly soon found, were there against their will. They had also been kidnapped, as it were, by press-gangs who seized them off their fishing boats, off merchant vessels, or even in the streets of their home towns, and forced them into the service of the Royal Navy. They were like men arbitrarily thrown into jail for an unspecified period and for no crime. Some endured the condition hopelessly, getting their only relief by joining in the slaughter of a sea fight, where all discipline was gone. Others constantly brooded on escape, deterred by the terror of a flogging if caught.

Some contrived to remain permanently drunk—not to

the extent that they could not handle their duties (for which they would be flogged), but to the degree of utterly dulling their minds. These endured cold, blows and hunger with doglike fortitude. They got the extra rum from their mates in return for taking over some of their work, or from the bosun's mates whom they helped to operate a sort of thieves' market on board, smuggling articles which could be sold at another port when opportunity arose. Another group found relief in religious services of a half-Christian and half-pagan kind. They gathered twice a day at the aft end of the gun deck and muttered prayers of submission and for protection. These men never swore and gave their rum ration to others. They were held in respect by their mates, for when action pended, they would ask them to pray for them.

The seamen in this cult were, all in all, better than the regular run of the men, being scrupulous in their duties out of a religious conviction rather than out of fear of punishment. The object of their worship was the Holy Star, which the men felt looked after them and would, in return for their devotion, see them all safe at last to their homes.

Only one man on the gun deck was there of his own accord—a bright, cheerful man in his middle twenties called Tom Redding. He was a rarity in the British Navy—a volunteer seaman, who came of a good farming family in one of the midland counties of England and had joined the frigate out of patriotism. He did not agree with the cruelties and harshness he saw around him, but he did his duties intelligently and well, holding that

England alone had the task of opposing the tyranny of Napoleon Bonaparte and as an Englishman he must play his part in this effort.

He had been offered promotion but refused, accepting only the position of head of his gun crew, which was the gun next to Manly's. The men respected him and listened to all he had to say on any subject. To a considerable degree he made them conscious of the entity beyond and behind their officers for which they fought—the entity called England, which was embodied in the flag the frigate flew and in painful, lovely, fleeting memories of little green fields and cottages with thatched roofs, or of the cobbled streets of London, hazy with smoke and the smell of sea coal.

The officers did not represent such things to the men. The captain, for instance, was merely the remote and merciless head of an organization of jailers. But Tom Redding represented such things, and Tom was given precedence in almost all matters of common concern. His crew, for example, went first to draw their kid of rations and got thus the better portions of salt beef ("salt horse," it was called, and with some reason) served by the cooks.

When it was time for the evening meal on his first day aboard out of the hold, Manly was sent by Weeks with the "kid," or wooden bucket, to draw the rations for his gun crew. This consisted of a greasy, greyish soupy mess, smelling very ripe, called "slumgullion." Its sole virtue was that it was hot, and it appeared to be plentiful. But when the men of the gun crew, constituting what was called a "mess," dipped into the kid with their sheath knives, the slumgullion was found to contain two large bones which made up at least a quarter of its volume. They complained and were told to fill up on ship's bread, of which they could have as much as they needed.

This sounded lavish, but the ship's bread was hard as a baked tile. None of the men had sound teeth. Being seamen, however, they found a way to make the bread edible by putting it on the deck in a cloth and rolling a twenty-pound shot over it. This after a while broke it down into pebble-sized pieces. These were put into the greyish stew and a portion served to each man in his pannikin. Manly could not eat his, hungry as he was. His appetite left him as the first spoonful neared his nose. He put some of the crumbs from the ship's bread or biscuit in his mouth, but found that his jaws ached before he could soften them up enough to swallow. Also, he found there were weevils in the biscuits, some in the form of grubs and others insects, and he decided he would sooner endure hunger than eat vermin.

That first meal on board, then, provided him with no nourishment but served to prepare him for many such to come. The next day he was so famished that he chewed his way through a ship's biscuit, weevils and all, and ate his full serving at the evening meal. Thereafter, he never missed a meal, but he was always hungry and especially hungry for anything sweet. A few dried raisins were served with the evening meal each Sunday, and he looked forward to their ration of rum.

The rum ration was issued twice a day from a cask placed at the break of the poop and guarded by two marines. The men were supposed to drink it down while standing before the cask, to prevent hoarding. But the hoarding went on anyway, and if a man did not wish to take his rum, a note was made of this and he was credited with one penny on the ship's accounts. Few applied for this credit. The crew of *Leopard* had last been paid three and a half years before, and they had come to believe they would never receive any more while the war lasted.

During his first days aboard, Manly was asked many questions about the reaction ashore to *Leopard* firing on and boarding *Chesapeake*. His opinion was earnestly sought and the Americans in the crew—fishermen and coastal seamen, for the most part—were the most eager of his questioners.

Manly said people seemed to think that there would be a war between the United States and Britain but his uncle did not think so. The prospect of a war pleased everybody. The Americans saw in it a chance either of liberation or of escape. The non-Americans saw a chance of action and an easy defeat of American ships, of which they had the poorest opinion—an opinion strongly reinforced by the surrender of *Chesapeake* without firing a shot.

Nobody on board *Leopard* wanted peace, and the crew was of the opinion that Manly's uncle was either a fool or a coward. Tom Redding, the volunteer, alone upheld Peter Treegate's view. One evening during dinner, while Manly was being lectured on the fact that war with the United States was inevitable because, as the seamen concerned said, "it'll give us a chance to get back what is rightly ours" (meaning the thirteen American colonies), Redding announced that he would be very surprised if the two countries went to war.

"Why so?" he was asked.

"Because," said Redding, "whatever their quarrels, Britain and America are both on the side of freedom. America, standing for freedom as she says she does, cannot ally herself with Napoleon, who is determined to enslave the world."

The thought that there might be no war between the two countries spread a certain amount of gloom around the gun deck. "We should have taken that *Chesapeake* frigate," said one of the hands. "We could have done it easy as kiss your hand."

"One day you're going to meet one of those Yankee frigates, broadside to broadside, and you're going to learn a thing or two," said another.

"Who says so?" asked the English sailor.

"Me," said the man who had spoken. He was one of the men claiming to be American who was taken off *Chesapeake*. "And I know what I'm talking about. I was with Decatur at Tripoli and I've seen a Yankee frigate fight."

"And I was a man-o'-war's man at Trafalgar," said another. "And I say there's no ship afloat can stand up to one of ours."

"Let's hope it does not come to such a test," said Redding. "When free men fall out, the whole world is the loser."

# 9

PETER Treegate, balked by the sailing of the frigate from
finding his nephew, went immediately to the one man
he knew who could help him—Theophilous Jones.
Jones, supplier of crews, insurer of cargoes, and the organizer of a shipping-intelligence service probably unique in
America, with agents in every port of the Atlantic, had the
resources to find and free the boy. So to him Peter Treegate went and related all he knew or could guess of
Manly's story.

"I can get him back to you," said Theophilous Jones
when he had finished. "It will take time and it will take
money. But it can be done and will be done."

"Whatever it costs, I will gladly pay," said Peter Treegate. "I am afraid for the boy. He has a certain stubborn-
ness that may cost him dear. He could suffer heavily for
that on a British frigate."

"He will learn," said Theophilous Jones. "We all do." Peter Treegate glanced at him sharply, recalling that the factor, who now had such influence in the world of shipping, had once been a slave in the French Island of Haiti and had secured his liberty in the revolt of slaves under Toussaint L'Ouverture. There were many rumors about the part he played in that revolt and the money he had obtained when he fled Haiti and made his way to the United States. But Theophilous Jones never spoke about these matters and seemed to enjoy the many rumors which circulated concerning him.

"My information is that *Leopard* will go to Halifax and from Halifax to the West Indies," said Mr. Jones. "Nothing can be done in Halifax. It is thick with naval agents. But the West Indian islands are another matter entirely. Something can certainly be done there."

"And in the meantime there is nothing I can do?" asked Peter Treegate. "Would it serve if I went to Halifax or the West Indies?"

"No," said Jones. "Remain here for the time being. But I would certainly seek an interview with Mr. Madison and request his aid. This will not be refused. An official request for the boy's return will, I am afraid, not succeed. But it should be attempted, for it will reduce the pressure on whatever I am able to do—unofficially." He paused and then said, changing the subject, "The British are becoming bold—bold beyond their normal boldness. What do you make of that, Mr. Treegate?"

"They are desperate," said Peter Treegate. "You know as well as I that not hundreds but thousands of their deserters are now serving on American ships. Their whole Navy is becoming inefficient through lack of men."

Jones took the snuffbox which he had received from the deserter Ratford and said, eyeing it with approval, "Would you care to guess how many British deserters are now serving on our ships?"

Peter Treegate shrugged. He had not come here to discuss this question, but he knew that Jones rarely entered into a conversation idly. "At random, two thousand," he said.

"It's nearer six thousand," said Jones. "In short, there are enough British deserters serving on our ships to man five first-raters in the British Navy. Or, to put the matter another way, Britain is deprived of five men-of-war as the result of the desertion of her seamen in this country. That is a heavy drain. No wonder her frigate captains have grown bold."

"*Leopard* firing on and then boarding *Chesapeake* is certainly the boldest action at sea I have heard of since the Tripoli Wars," said Peter Treegate.

"It ran the risk of war," said Mr. Jones.

"That is what the British would like," said Peter Treegate. "But there must be no war. We cannot win it. We can only lose by it. We have no navy to put up against Britain's and war would only mean the end of our trade, the sealing of our ports and perhaps the reoccupation of our land."

"The boldness of the British suggests to me what it suggests to you—that Britain wants war," said Jones. "Are you aware, Mr. Treegate, that whether this country goes to war or not is a decision that now lies largely in your hands?"

"In my hands?" cried Peter Treegate, utterly surprised.

"Yours and nobody else's," said Mr. Jones. "If on top of the *Chesapeake* episode you were to publish widely the fact that an American boy, sailing on Chesapeake Bay, had been seized and pressed into service on the same British frigate that attacked *Chesapeake,* not all the diplomacy of Mr. Madison or Mr. Jefferson or Gallatin or anyone could withstand the furor demanding instant hostilities between this country and Great Britain. The nation is raging now. Publicize this further outrage and war is inevitable."

"I have no intention of publicizing the matter at all," said Peter Treegate.

"Excellent," said Mr. Jones. "That being the case, if you will take my advice and go to Mr. Madison privately, you will find him, I am sure, utterly zealous in doing everything that lies in the government's power to effect the return of your nephew. A last word to the wise, Mr. Treegate, which I trust you will not resent."

"What is it?"

"There is likely to be a considerable decrease in the seaborne commerce of the United States. That commerce is, in fact, likely to come to a standstill. I would advise you to keep as many ships as possible abroad, with instructions not to return to American ports after October. And I would advise you to cut down on your warehousing and wharfing expenses and sell such vessels as cannot immediately be employed in overseas trade."

Mr. Treegate considered this information for some seconds and then said, "You think the British will blockade our ports?"

Mr. Jones smiled. "No, Mr. Treegate," he said. "I think Mr. Jefferson will blockade our ports." That remarkable statement concluded the interview.

It was not difficult for Peter Treegate to secure an interview with Secretary of State Madison. He was well-known as one of the biggest shipowners and importers and exporters of New England, and the Republican cause headed by Jefferson and Madison was anxious for support of such men as he. Congress was not then in session and would not meet again until October, and the President had not thought fit to call an emergency session. Indeed, with the country clamoring for war, an emergency session of the Congress was the last thing the President wanted since such a session would result in the nation being plunged into war with Britain, a war which was being demanded on every side. Such a war was the subject of three distinct orations that Peter Treegate had to listen to outside of taverns while waiting for new horses on his way to Washington. He found on that journey that a new slogan was popular everywhere: "Free Trade and Sailor's Rights."

Mr. Madison received Peter Treegate two days after he arrived in the dusty village of Washington, where the President's official residence (by no means complete) now stood, and where the building which was to house the Congress was being erected in a low-lying marsh which bred myriads of mosquitoes.

There was as yet no official residence for the State Department, and this was housed in a large and ugly building some distance along a dusty road from the President's mansion. On the day of his appointment, Peter Treegate tied his horse to a railing in front of the gaunt building in which the nation's foreign affairs were conducted, and after knocking at the door, he was admitted by an elderly Negro slave. The slave conducted him, after a slight delay, to an upstair's study, where Mr. Madison sat at a table like a schoolboy delayed over his lessons.

The physical contrast between the two men was sharp, for Treegate stood well over six feet and Mr. Madison was scarcely five and a half feet tall and so slightly built that it seemed that all growth had been arrested when he was twelve years of age.

In his letter requesting this interview, Peter Treegate had made no mention of the kidnapping of his nephew. He told the Secretary of State of this now, and Madison, who had the reputation of never being angry, was appalled at the story. "This is piracy," he exclaimed. "There is no difference between this and what we endured for many years at the hands of the Barbary powers. I will write immediately to our minister in London and instruct him to press for immediate release of the boy.

"I do not understand this at all, Mr. Treegate. I can understand to a degree the *Chesapeake* incident—understand it, mind you, not condone it. Are you sure that there were not other circumstances involved in the seizure of your nephew? His seizure by a picket boat seems utterly callous and haphazard."

"I know of no circumstances other than that the boy was boating on Chesapeake Bay with a man called Coffin.

It might be that it was Coffin they wanted, and they took the boy as being a witness to the seizure of Coffin. I have made inquiries concerning Coffin and he is not a British deserter. He was born in this country and had never ventured abroad nor served on a foreign vessel."

Madison gave Mr. Treegate a calculating look. Politically, the two were of opposing parties. Treegate, coming from New England, with extensive mercantile interest, was a Federalist, opposed to the pro-French, anti-British leanings of Jefferson's Republicans.

"Have you written to the press concerning this matter, Mr. Treegate?" he asked. He put the question as if the answer was of trifling importance.

"No," said the other. "At the present moment, I do not wish to force the hand of the government."

"That was wise of you, Mr. Treegate," said Madison smoothly. "Governments, in matters of crisis, must not react under pressure of a national emotion uninstructed by the facts. Oh, do not take me wrong. I refer to the military and economic facts. And those facts are such that it is the President's opinion that no greater disaster could befall this nation than a war with Great Britain at this time."

"The President's opinion?" said Mr. Treegate.

"In which, of course, I wholeheartedly concur," said Mr. Madison hurriedly. "It is the policy of the government, avoiding war, to defend our own coasts and to expend its funds on defensive rather than offensive armament. We must not let popular clamor force us into hostilities.

"You will understand that if we embark on an extensive program of rearmament—building ships of the line, for instance, and a vast frigate fleet—Britain might well interpret this as an intention to attack. But if our naval effort is limited to defensive armament, to the construction of a vast fleet of gunboats which can protect our harbors but certainly could not launch an attack, then it would be clear to Britain and to others that we pose no menace to them, that we intend only to defend ourselves and can and will do so, and this must certainly dissuade them from launching any attack on us."

"Your gunboats will not be able to protect our harbors, Mr. Madison," said Peter Treegate.

"At the present moment, no," said Madison. "There are not enough of them. But when they are present in all our principal harbors, in swarms, then they will be able to protect us. That, you will remember, was our experience in the Tripoli Wars. The Algerian powers relied almost entirely on small gunboats, which attacked our frigates in clouds and prevented us for many years from penetrating their harbor defenses."

"On that head," said Mr. Treegate, "I would call to your mind three points which should not be overlooked. The first is that the Mediterranean is a very different body of water from the Atlantic, and gunboats that can operate in the calm of the Mediterranean cannot operate in the Atlantic swells. The second point is that at the height of the Tripoli Wars we were never able to muster more than a few frigates, which is not to be compared with the naval might Britain could send against us if she so chose. The third point is that, despite the favorable Mediterranean conditions for the use of gunboats, and despite the paucity of our own naval strength compared with that of Britain, we won the Tripoli Wars, Mr. Madison. The gunboats of our enemy were of no avail in the end."

"What is your advice?" asked the Secretary.

"You will not like it," said Mr. Treegate.

"That is often the case with valuable advice," said Madison smiling. "Tell me your opinion, pray."

"The greater part of our revenue comes from exporting and importing," said Mr. Treegate. "The greater part of that, although we are opening a trade with China and the Levant, comes from Britain.

"Given those facts, you can readily deduce my advice. It is that we should, by hints of aid and favor, play Britain against France and France against Britain while remaining neutral as long as we may. Each of those powers, suspecting that we will come to the aid of the other, will handle us more respectfully than at present. When that game is played out, as it must be, we should choose sides, and the side we should choose is the one that provides us with our greatest market—Britain."

"Come, sir," said Mr. Madison. "Do you advise that we ally ourselves with the same King George whose tyranny you and I helped to overthrow? And in so doing become the enemy of France, who alone in all the world came to our aid in our struggle for liberty?"

"Yes. I do so advise," said Peter Treegate. "For, whatever the temporary abuses of power under past and present governments of Britain, the whole direction of that government through history, taking a long view, has been government by law; which means government with control over the governors. But France has no such heritage. She may speak of freedom, but her people have less freedom now than when the last Louis ruled at Versailles. You must not mistake a moment in time for the whole flood of history. Hostility to England, not love of liberty, brought France to our aid in the Revolution. That is something that should not be forgotten."

The two men, so vastly different physically and mentally, stared at each other in silence. A French clock with a swinging pendulum sounded the hour from the mantelpiece, and somewhere in the garden the squawking of a blue jay shattered the peace of the afternoon.

"I will convey your views to Mr. Jefferson," said Madison dryly. "He will be interested in hearing them." He rose and held out a tiny hand. "You have my word that no effort will be spared to bring about the speedy return of your nephew," he said.

On that they parted.

# 10

*Leopard* made a fast passage to Halifax. Like a sleek black hunting cat headed for its lair, she paused only twice in the long run north: once to chase a French sloop, which gave her the slip in the northern fogs; and again to board a New York schooner returning from Europe and search for "deserters."

Two men were taken from her crew on the grounds that they spoke with a Welsh accent and must therefore be British. Their shipmates could do nothing to save them and they were put aboard *Leopard*. Then the frigate plunged on through a searing westerly that rolled her leeward gunports under and flung icy spray up to her topmasts. The "long twenties," which constituted her principal broadside, strained at their breechings and had to have double tackles put on them. The gun deck was a tilted, slippery, roaring confusion of darkness and water, and the one hot meal of the day was often eaten with a dollop of seawater for sauce.

Manly Treegate spent the first two days at sea in complete misery, and this was replaced by a deep and stubborn anger such as he had never experienced before. This was too intense to last, and it was in turn replaced by a dogged acceptance of his fate and an equally dogged determination to desert the frigate whenever he had a chance.

He learned the way of the ship fast. The captain and his officers—sailing master, first, second, and third lieutenants—he saw only occasionally and they never spoke to him. The men he got his orders from were the bosun's mates, who were the taskmasters on every job that had to be performed aboard. With these bosun's mates there were always the midshipmen—officially in charge but learning from the bosun's mates and the seamen.

There were half a dozen midshipmen, and they wore jackets to distinguish them from the ship's boys. It came as a surprise to Manly that the officers were as hard on the midshipmen as they were on the crew. They were expected to be familiar with every aspect of the ship's work. They got schooling from the sailmaker, from the master gunner, from the carpenter, from the bosuns and from the sailing master, and they stood watches as well, so that they were always short of sleep. Prynne, the one who had hit Manly on his first day aboard, was the worst of the lot. He had a streak of meanness in him which he took pleasure in satisfying, and Manly learned to keep out of his way, or, if he was present, to keep especially busy.

At Halifax, Manly met with a big disappointment, for no one was allowed shore leave and those who had to go ashore on ship's business were under the eye of an armed officer. The frigate refilled her water casks, took on powder and shot, replaced her fore topmast, which had been damaged in previous action, and in four days headed due south, her destination being the West Indies. In all that time Manly saw Halifax only from the ship and worked like a dog getting the stores stowed as they came aboard. In harbor he was assigned for a while to the powder hold, where, under the eye of the master gunner, he learned to make up paper cartridges of powder for the ship's guns. The powder hold was entirely lined with felt and had, then, a menacing silence about it, for the felt muffled all noise. Kegs of powder were stored in high racks all around the walls. The powder from them was carefully measured by the master gunner onto a square of rough paper. Then the paper was rolled to make a cylindrical package, the ends being folded in a particular manner and the package or cartridge being roughly the size of the bore of the guns. These cartridges were stored in leather buckets, and in action it was Manly's job, as one of the ship's powder boys, to keep his gun supplied with buckets of cartridges, carrying them from the powder hold to the gun. The powder hold was in the lowest part of the ship, amidships. It was lit by a lantern set in the wall and cut off from the hold by a pane of glass. The pane of glass could not be removed, so the lantern had to be serviced from outside the powder hold.

The master gunner had a measure which he was supposed to use to dole out the exact amount of powder for each cartridge, the amount changing according to the weight of shot. There was also a wooden paddle for getting the powder out of the barrels. But the master gunner preferred to measure the powder with his hands, and his only use for the wooden paddle was to hit the powder boys with it when they did anything he judged foolish.

Now and again, particularly if any of the midshipmen were present (for they also had to learn the business of making cartridges), the master gunner would give a lecture on gunpowder and its curious characteristics. He spoke of it as a living substance which had to be closely studied. It was affected by moonlight, he assured them, having less force in the full of the moon. In action by moonlight, the boys should put the leather buckets of cartridges in the shadows for the best effect. Seawater in moderate amounts did not hurt the gunpowder, he held, but fresh water ruined it, taking the strength out of the saltpeter which was one of its constituents. Powder that was very black, containing then an unusual amount of charcoal, was slow-burning but had the most force. The grey powder exploded immediately but not with such great effect.

The master gunner said that a pinch of gunpowder taken once a week would keep a man healthy, and he said that when the boys took the buckets of cartridges up on deck during action, they were to hug them to their chests with both arms around them to protect them from stray shot or from flaming ropes, sails, and other debris of battle.

"Serve your own gun," he said. "Nobody else's. But if it is out of action, look for a gun that has lost its powder boy. There's a powerful number of them killed, being kept too busy to time the enemy's broadsides and so take cover."

"Last action we lost two," said Midshipman Prynne. "Found Lockley by the port cathead. Think it was Lockley. Insubordinate little pup. Served him right." He looked straight at Manly, but Manly, warned by experience, avoided the look and went on working on the cartridge he was making.

"I was going to have him flogged," continued Prynne. "For dumb insolence. Do you know what dumb insolence is, Treegate?"

Directly addressed, Manly raised his eyes and said, "No, sir."

"Dumb insolence is exactly what you were doing then. Continuing with your work when addressed by an officer. Master gunner, send him to me when you are through with him. I have work for him to do."

"Aye aye, sir," said the master gunner.

And so, at the end of that session, Manly was put to work exchanging the shot among the guns, carrying the twenty-pound shot from number-one gun to number twenty and from number twenty to number one. He was kept at this utterly senseless task for two hours, which, because this included the mealtime, meant he got nothing to eat that day. But the boy from the next gun to his, who served with Redding, saved him a piece of boiled beef. His name was Roberts. He had flaming red hair and very white skin, heavily splotched with red freckles. He had a special hatred for Midshipman Prynne.

"Thank you," said Manly when Roberts gave him the piece of beef.

"Don't let Prynne see you eat it," said Roberts.

"Who was Lockley?" asked Manly, wolfing down the beef.

"He was my friend," said Roberts. "Same crew as you. Save the bone. I'm making a ship."

Later he showed Manly the ship he was making—a lovely little bomb ketch, the hull, masts, guns and decks all carved of bone and smoothed to the texture of ivory.

"I'm going to give it to my dad," he said. "He lives in Nottingham." Manly's schooling had gone far enough for him to identify Nottingham as not being an English seaport town. It was odd that, coming from an inland town, Roberts should be at sea. "Me and Lockley ran away to Liverpool," Roberts explained. "Just for a lark, and that's where the press-gang caught us. Five years ago."

"And you never got home since?"

"No. And won't until the war's over. That will be soon, they say. We smashed them at the Nile and at Copenhagen and at Trafalgar." Despite the fact that he had been forced into the Navy and subject to unceasing brutality, he seemed proud. "We can beat anything we meet on the sea," he added. Manly made no comment on this.

At Halifax, *Leopard* took on sixty tons of shot, twenty tons of powder and sixteen tons of water, in addition to other stores. She also took aboard additional spars and two extra small boats, so that she was laden beyond her design and sailed deep, ten inches below her lines, one of the bosuns said. This made her slow, and to speed her up on the voyage south to the West Indies, more canvas was piled on her yards and was kept flying even in heavy weather. She got out of Nova Scotia in a northeasterly which served excellently, and in two days she was off New York, though two hundred miles to sea. Then, reaching the northerly edge of the Gulf Stream two days later, the wind slewed around into what the seamen called a "dead mussler," straight out of the south.

"Hands to sheets and braces," came the cry, and Manly's watch being on deck, he tailed on behind his crew on the main-yard brace. The captain himself stood beside the quartermasters—there were two at the wheel— eyeing the rippling topsails. The sailing master shouted, "Sheet home all." The great network of lines which stretched from various points on the deck to the slings on the ends of the yards and to the corners of the frigate's twenty sails tautened, blocks shrilled and clacked, and yards and sails swung around to lie more fore and aft along the ship. The quartermasters let the wheel slip through their hands, spoke by spoke, until the luff or leading edge of the main upper topgallant trembled.

"How's her head?" asked the captain.

"Southwest by west."

The sailing master and the captain exchanged glances and the sailing master shouted, "Harden her up, bosun, put some ginger in it." A bosun's mate brought a knotted rope smartly across Manly's shoulders, hard enough to knock the breath out of him. "Heave till she cries out," he shouted, and brought the rope down again, this time on another back. The men heaved on the braces and sheets, tightening the sails even further so the frigate might lie a trifle closer to the wind. The full watch on deck numbered sixty men. Even so, the watch below was routed up to bear a hand until the quartermaster was able to report a course of southwest.

"Make it so," said the captain, and the yards and sheets were belayed and the watch dispersed to whatever shelter could be found about the deck.

The weather thickened that afternoon, a shroud of fog steaming up off the surface of the ocean. The sea turned a dirty grey, and where a wave crested, the foam was yellow instead of white. The wind increased and the fog flitted past her in nightmare globs—now so thick that it was impossible to see the width of the deck, and now thinning until the long bowsprit straining under the weight of the headsails could be seen flailing against the grey sea and the grey air.

Closehauled and carrying so much canvas, *Leopard* heeled sharply, but having many tons of supplies in her holds, she only rarely dipped her gunports, now wedged shut and with the guns run back in double breechings.

Manly was sent to the foretop as lookout and up there was surprised to find the fog very much thinner, so that he could at times see up to a mile about him. But such was the peculiarity of this Gulf Stream mist that many times he could not see the deck below him, and even the vast expanse of the forecourse melted into nothingness at times, leaving him perched in the swirls of grey with the feeling that he was flying through the air with nothing solid anywhere about him.

A hundred feet above the deck, the heeling of the frigate was greatly magnified. From below came the roar and hiss of the sea as *Leopard,* hard pressed, smashed from one wave to another. All about him was a world of grey mist, and above the smashing of the frigate into the head seas he could hear faint consoling sounds, little whimpers and pipings of wind on sail edge and on rigging, which lulled him half to sleep. When he put his head close to the mast, he could hear a deep rumble from it caused by the turbulence of the wind flying past its bulk.

He was not afraid at being so high and alone, for he had climbed masts which, although smaller, were far more slender than this. After an hour at his post he began to feel chilled and his limbs were cramped. He considered climbing to the lower topgallant yard and working his way out along the footrope to warm up, but he suspected he would be punished if he moved. He stretched and stood up to see what rigging was available for the venture, however, and caught for a second a flash of white to windward just off the end of the topsail yard.

"Sail ho!" he shouted. "Sail ho, broad on the starboard bow." Then he saw it again, not just a white flash but a whole tower of canvas in the swirling fog, and he knew what it was from the size—a ship of the line, bearing down on them from the west and scarcely a mile off. It

99

had been seen now by someone else, for he heard from below the short angry bark of a wooden rattle and then the rumble of a drum as *Leopard*'s crew were beat to quarters. He reached for the backstay to slide to the deck, tingling with excitement at the prospect of action.

# 11

A decision had to be made immediately whether to run from the strange ship or turn and meet her, and that decision depended on whether she was French or British. If French, *Leopard* must flee, for no frigate could fight a two-decker, whose heavy broadside could demolish her at one blow. The ship had seen them in the same moment and had altered course to intercept. But that action itself gave no clue to her nationality. While *Leopard*'s gun crews removed the tampions from their pieces, and while the powder boys, Manly among them, scurried to bring buckets of cartridges to their guns, Sir Thomas Carroll, *Leopard*'s captain, himself went to the main topgallant, scurrying up the rigging very handily, with a glass under his arm to examine the strange ship.

He was up and down faster than his crew thought possible and gave his verdict.

"French," he said. "We must run. Keep her hard on the wind and run the guns out to weather. There'll be twenty of the cat for you if you luff her, quartermaster. Keep her full and by. Send a hand to call the luff of the main topgallant."

The quartermaster at the wheel would normally watch the leading edge or luff of this sail to see that it was full and not backing. But, in the foggy conditions, he could not see it, and would then have to be told. A man scrambled up the rigging for this duty, a reef was shaken out of the lower topgallants, all staysails set, and *Leopard,* smashing from wave to wave, fought to windward for her very life. The French two-decker threshed along in chase, not quite in range for her long twenty-four-pounders. Running the windward guns out had the effect of helping *Leopard* stand up to the great weight of canvas she was now carrying, with the reefs out of her lower topgallants.

The gun deck was now manned and every piece ready for action. Forty twenty-pounders with seven men to each gun meant over two hundred eighty men crowded in the gun deck where there was not room to stand. Lanterns were passed out by the bosun to reduce the darkness, for none of the ports were open yet. The lanterns swung from the deck beams, illuminating the bare backs and arms and grim faces of the men. The concentration of so many men in so restricted a space, the lack of ventilation and the burning of the lanterns soon set up a heavy fog, and permission was granted to ease a couple of gunports and freshen the air below.

Aft, the Holy Star men were holding a service around their piece and snatches of their petitions came to

Manly crouched by the garlands of roundshot by his gun. ". . . Steadfast in faith . . . servants of the Star . . . see us safe . . ."

Second Lieutenant Marston, the gunnery officer, passed along inspecting each piece for readiness. He extinguished the slow matches burning in their tubs, indicating that action was not expected immediately. This had the effect of reducing the coughing among the gun crew. When he got to the Holy Star men, they stopped their prayer until he had gone by. Then they resumed, though the rules called for absolute silence once the crew had been beat to quarters so that orders could be plainly heard.

For a while, only the tumble and roar of the water around the hull, the prayers of the men and the creaking of the guns in their breechings as *Leopard* plunged from wave to wave interrupted the gun-deck silence. Then there came a heavy dull report, followed by a surprising hiss, as if a hot poker had been put into a bucket of water.

Prynne, who was standing to the rear of Manly's gun, tried to look unconcerned, but the anxiety showed in his face.

"Frogs are firing high," he said. There was no need for anyone to add the remark that the French ship was within range now. A minute later there was another report, but this time no shot was heard. The round had gone into the sea, falling short. More followed, at carefully spaced intervals, so that it occurred to Manly that the French gunnery officer must be firing with a watch in his hand.

Three shots went over the frigate, two missed. Following the last, the frigate trembled under a heavy blow and there was a great rushing of feet overhead. Then there was a tremendous blow on the deck overhead and immediately the sounds of the water around the hull changed. The frigate slowed, and Manly did not need anyone to tell him that one of her yards had been shot away.

It was the fore lower topgallant yard that had fallen. The sling had been cut by a lucky shot, for no aim at any particular target was possible in the heavy sea. The sail fluttered and flapped, making more furor than the cannon fire, and flung the yard. One end of the yard crashed into the forestaysail stay and brought that down, and then the whole tangle of yard, sail, halyards, sheets, braces and stays tumbled to the deck, much of the sail going under the forefoot of the frigate and slowing her further in the water.

Many things happened immediately. The bosun had a dozen men on the fallen yard like starving rats on a piece of cheese, rigging a new sling and passing a new halyard to get the yard aloft again. The sailmaker, with one glance at the sail, cut it away and tumbled another up on deck in short order. The sail was set to the spar even before the rigging of the sling was completed. The ship's clerk came scurrying down to Marston with orders to ready the starboard broadside, and while the bosun and sailmaker's gangs were tailing on the topgallant halyard to sweat the yard aloft on its jackstay, the captain made the decision to turn and fight.

"You must tack, if you please," he said to the sailing master. "Give her a broadside as we cross her bow. As soon as it is delivered, be ready to put her back at my command on the original tack."

"Aye aye, sir," said the sailing master, and repeated these orders to the quartermaster, who had heard them anyway. A ship's boy came to the break of the poop and presented Mr. Marston's compliments and the report that the starboard broadside was ready to fire. The sailing master presented his compliments in return and said it was the captain's wish that the starboard broadside be fired at the most opportune moment immediately after the frigate had crossed the wind. It was the captain's desire to fall back on the original tack immediately after the broadside. This latter information was important. By judging the firing of the guns nicely, Marston could help the frigate tack again with the recoil, where otherwise she might hang in stay.

All was now ready. The fog had thinned to a mere mist, and the loss of her topgallant had so slowed *Leopard* that the Frenchman was scarcely a mile away and coming up fast.

"Luff up," said the sailing master, and the wheel was opened smartly to windward. The foreyards backed and the frigate seemed to stop in the weltering ocean, and she became, though only for a moment, more upright. She rose with a corkscrew motion on the back of a vast roller, flinging skyward like a rearing horse, and in that second Marston brought down his upraised arm and twenty smoldering matches were touched to twenty quills in the touchholes of the guns of the starboard broadside. In a second they detonated almost in unison and with appalling effect. It seemed to Manly that the whole ship had blown up and its side had been exploded clean out of it.

The guns were jerked back against their breechings as if they weighed not tons but ounces. There was one tremendous flash of flame and then the whole gun deck and everybody on it disappeared in smoke.

A wet swab was thrust down the smoking barrel of Manly's gun, producing a surprising spurt of smoke from the touchhole. Manly passed another cartridge to the swabber's mate, who tore the paper with his teeth and then pushed the cartridge with its powder into the barrel. It was important to break the paper so that there was loose powder in the breech; otherwise, there would be a misfire. A felt pad was rammed down behind the cartridge, the gun elevated, a twenty-pound shot dropped down the barrel and held there with another felt plug, rammed home hard, and the gun was run out and ready to fire again. All this was done in just over a minute. To signal that the gun was ready to fire, the gun pointer, who was also the crew chief, raised his arm in the air. Within two minutes, while the smoke still swirled about her gun deck, *Leopard* was ready to deliver a second broadside from her batteries. Nobody on the gun deck could see the effect of the first broadside as the horizon there was limited to the next wave. In any case, hardly was the broadside delivered when, with the foreyards still backed, the helmsman, at a yell from the sailing master, spun the wheel downwind. *Leopard* hesitated, bobbing and rolling horribly in the water, slamming her guns forward and back against their breechings. Then, slowly, she fell off to larboard, the backed foreyards swung over with a thump that shook her rigging and she took off across the grey ocean in a spurt of speed that flung the spray up to her main yards. The ruse, for such it was, had worked. As soon as *Leopard* had come into the wind, the Frenchman had followed suit, taking more time, however, for being a bigger ship, she was slower in stays. *Leopard*'s broadside struck her high, as she came to the wind, with maximum exposure. Her main and forecourse were riddled with holes, which expanded in a moment into vast tears. The gaff on the driver on her mizzen came tumbling down to hang like a club over the poop.

The Frenchman was hurt but by no means crippled. But she had been outwitted. She fell off on the new tack and her captain was chagrined to see, when his sails were drawing again, the two ships now on opposite tacks and pulling rapidly apart from each other, *Leopard* having resumed her original course. He had but one remedy immediately available and he tried it. He called for a larboard broadside, and some seconds later (for the French guns were much worse served than the British) a ragged volley erupted from the two-decker and half a ton of shot, visible for a second like a flight of geese (for the fog had lifted), flung across the grey water in the direction of the British frigate.

*Leopard* had her stern to the broadside and the range was a mile and a half. But *Leopard* was unlucky. Her fore and main topmasts were hit and dangled down like broken wings. Every sail she had spread except the staysails was ripped with holes. The bosun, the carpenter and all hands not assigned to specific duty flung themselves furiously on the damaged masts. There was a dead marine lying in a huddle on the stump of the topmast and the bosun flung the body, without caring, into the sea below. There was no question of sending up new topmasts at sea. All that could be done was clear away the tangle so as to get the other rigging free and the other sails drawing efficiently. The frigate was eased a full point off the wind so she could pick up some of the speed she lost with her topmasts. There was no time for the Frenchman to try a second broadside. She swung around in pursuit and lobbed a shot or two with her bow chaser, while *Leopard*'s captain eyed her through his glass and considered the various ways in which he might get more speed from the frigate.

There was a variety of things he could do. He could tumble his battery of twenty thirty-two-pounder carronades on the forecastle and quarterdeck overboard. That would lighten the frigate by a hundred tons, which would raise her half an inch in the water and would give her a knot more speed. He could dump half his water and all his boats, which would also increase speed, but not as much. He could knock the chocks out of the lower masts so that they leaned forward a trifle, which would bring him some increase of speed. Or he could have the carpenter saw through every other frame of the ship, which would make her hull more supple and also produce an increase of speed. But all these possibilities, while adding to his speed, would take time and cripple his ship, and he wondered whether there was not something else that might be done faster.

He turned to survey the tangle of rigging and spars and sails which the bosun and his crew were now lowering to the deck from above, and he knew what to do.

"Pass the word for the bosun," he told his clerk, and the clerk darted off to come back with Mr. Grogham, the bosun, worried about what he had done that was wrong.

"Mr. Grogham," said the captain, "I am going to harden up, and I think we can lie half a point closer to the wind than the frog. Meanwhile, I want you to get out all the spare hawser, cable, lines, small stuff we have on board, together with the topmast spars and their rigging and yards, and bring it all to the spar deck. Have the sailmaker bring also all his old sails. I want that whole conglomeration, Mr. Grogham, dropped over the side, in as much of a maze as you can contrive and with the yawl at the end of it. Have the master gunner put a keg of powder in an old sail in the yawl with a fuse set—" he glanced aft—"for twenty minutes."

"Aye aye, sir," said the bosun.

"How long will this take you?" asked Sir Thomas.

"All the spare stores?" asked the bosun.

"Half of them," said Sir Thomas.

"Twenty minutes, sir," said the bosun.

"See to it, then."

Bosuns are by nature tidy people, and it surprised the captain to see what a tangle Grogham could contrive out of the material at his disposal. He had apparently as great a talent for confusion as for tidiness, and when the bosun got the signal, he began to lower over the side an enormous tangle of chain, spars, sails, blocks, nettings, hammocks, barrels, buckets—all lashed together with cables and ropes. The frigate's yawl, tied to one end of this ungodly collection and with a tub of powder on a long fuse under the stern sheets, was heaved bodily overboard first, and then the whole shambles was put over the side. The bigger items like sails and spars floated apart, and the hawsers and cables connecting them tended to sink, so that the fact that all were connected could not be observed from a hundred yards away—too late for the Frenchman to alter course. The ship's yawl floated forlornly in all this jumble, and it was a reasonable hope that the Frenchman would think the frigate had dumped the dunnage and her yawl to lighten her. Sir Thomas Carroll, *Leopard*'s captain, hoped the Frenchman would delay long enough to pick up the yawl, which was a good boat, but he had even better luck than that. The man-of-war swept along into the middle of the debris, and the tangle of cables and hawsers was caught under her forefoot and then, by the pressure of the water, driven under her keel. The yawl slipped back alongside the hull, settled next to the rudderstock for a moment, and then the keg of powder blew up. Sir Thomas, watching the French vessel through his glass, saw her swing slowly up into the wind and her foreyards back. Her rudder, then, was damaged; to what extent he did not particularly care. He hesitated for a moment, evaluating the prospect of crossing the bow or stern of the crippled Frenchman and giving her a broadside which might cripple her further. His orders were to join the Jamaica convoy now assembling at Kingston and not risk his frigate. Almost with a sigh, he snapped his long glass shut, handed it to his clerk and went below. *Leopard,* safe again, sped on southward, flashing through the grey sea, with plenty of time for her crew to repair the damage done to her.

# 12

In the Cape of San Martin on the north coast of Haiti the privateer *Bonne Chance* lay at anchor, while her crew, at their leisure, lolled in whatever shade they could find aboard or, shouting happily, swam and dived in the pale green water, which was so clear that every link of the anchor chain to the bottom, forty feet below, could be distinctly seen.

They were blacks and mulattoes for the most part—freed slaves, then—but their captain was a Frenchman and one of the few who had managed to escape the slaughter of the whites on the island which followed the slave revolt. His name was Rougecroix.

*Bonne Chance* carried French colors and served the cause of France. She was fast and big—110 feet between uprights—and she carried a main battery of sixteen eighteen-pounders and a smaller battery on her quarterdeck of six thirty-two-pounder carronades. Also, *Bonne Chance* was a lucky ship. Stealing like a ferret along that chain of West Indian Islands which stretched like a loose string of beads from the Dry Tortugas off Florida to Trinidad off the coast of Venezuela, she had taken to date thirty million francs in prize money.

Jean Rougecroix had chosen his present anchorage carefully. The cove faced east, and this being October, the northeast trades had been replaced by weak westerlies. In back of the bay were two ridges of hills separated by a lush valley and leading inland to vast, shrouded mountain peaks. In the valley between these two hills the westerly wind, when it was blowing, gained speed, reaching a brisk fifteen knots at the mouth of the cove, though where he was anchored only a slight breeze blew. So, if he had to leave in a hurry, he could slip his cable and be sure of a hefty following wind to get him out to sea—while anything coming in for him from seaward could never make it into the cove against a head wind. Happy in this knowledge, Captain Jean Rougecroix relaxed in his cabin and thought about the sailing of the British Jamaica convoy late in October. This would be the first convoy of the season, and it was scheduled to leave Kingston, Jamaica, around the full of the moon, according to his information.

The hurricane season would then be over for the year. The convoy would take the Windward Passage between Cuba and Haiti to get into the Atlantic and, riding the Gulf Stream eastward, head for England. Seventy sail, he had been told. There would be a guard of two British ships of the line—*Centurion* and *Formidable;* and three frigates—*Leopard, Roebuck* and *Peacock.* The ships of the line were not his principal concern, for they were vast, lumbering vessels, floating fortresses which could attain no great speed until half a gale was blowing. In light winds they could hardly maintain steerage. The frigates were another matter. They were not quite as fast as *Bonne Chance* (built in Baltimore, seized in Haiti), but they were fast enough and they outgunned her. Still, he was not without allies. The French two-decker *Indomptable* would handle the frigates, and he had already agreed with her captain on a plan for luring at least one of the frigates away from the convoy. The two-decker lay on the other side of the Tortugas awaiting the convoy.

Rougecroix had a chart of the Windward Passage before him. He had studied it a score of times and he fell to studying it again, thinking of the mountains of Cuba to the west and of Haiti to the east and hoping for a westerly wind, very light, which would demand that the whole convoy stay close to the Haiti coast. That would suit his purpose well.

There was a sudden whirring of big wings, and a blue-and-yellow parrot, as big as a hen, plumped down on the chart on the table and peered at Rougecroix out of its tawny eyes. He held out his fist, and the parrot, having inspected it, stepped onto his hand and then walked up his arm to rest on his shoulder, where it started preening.

There was a bump on the side of the ship and Rougecroix was on his feet in a moment, for he knew a boat had come alongside. He eased a drawer in the table open and took out a two-barreled pistol, which he put on the table-top, and then Simon, his mulatto mate, appeared in the companionway of the cabin, blocking out the light for a moment.

"Gubu," he said. "He has a message and a letter."

"Holy blood," said Rougecroix, "I told him not to come to me here." Simon moved aside and Gubu came in. He was a big black—bigger than Simon, who was no small man—and dressed in remarkable fashion. He wore the blue dress coat of an officer of the Fifteenth Chausseurs, the white frogging on the front in tatters and one of the epaulets, with its white tassels, dangling down the sleeve. The buttons of this coat were gone, so that it fell open, revealing his huge chest, which was sprinkled with white hair, for he was an older man. There were dark lines of shiny skin across his chest and stomach made by the lash, for Gubu had been a slave, and being slow in his wits and stubborn, he had often been flogged.

Below the jacket was a pair of dirty white breeches which had also been part of a French officer's uniform. The buttons at the knees were long gone, so these flapped open. The breeches were kept in place by a piece of rope. To complete the uniform, Gubu wore a cavalryman's saber slung on a bandoleer across his shoulders. His hair was curly and sprinkled with white and peeped out from beneath a sort of turban fashioned from bright green cloth.

"Anybody see you?" asked Rougecroix. "I told you not to come for me here. Nobody is supposed to come to me here." He spoke in the curious mixture of French, Spanish and African which was the common language of this portion of the West Indian Islands. Gubu took no notice of the question.

"Give me one hundred francs," he said.

"Thunder," snapped Rougecroix. "What for?"

"I have a message and a letter. Give me one hundred francs." He held out a hand on which the skin was as thick and as tough as that on the soles of his feet. Rougecroix opened a strongbox under his bunk, took out some coins, counted them carefully and gave them to Gubu, who turned each one over to examine the inscription before he put them in the pocket of his trousers. Then, from the interior of the French officer's coat, he took out a soiled envelope which he gave to Rougecroix. There was no address on it, but there was a seal on the back in black wax. The imprint on the seal was of an overseer holding a lash, so Rougecroix knew the message came from Theophilous Jones in Norfolk. He put it aside to open later.

"What's the message?" asked Rougecroix.

"You give me that parrot," said Gubu.

"You've been paid already," said Rougecroix.

"Give me the parrot or you don't get the message. Can he talk?"

"No," said Rougecroix, answering this question despite himself.

"You got to cut his tongue down the middle," said Gubu. He reached out a horny finger to the parrot, which bit on it hard enough to draw blood, though Gubu did not flinch. Satisfied that the finger was not inimical, the parrot stepped from Rougecroix's shoulder to Gubu's hand and then continued its preening on his wrist.

116

"The convoy sailed yesterday noon," said Gubu, stroking the parrot. "It will be in the Passage tonight. There's two ships of the line and three frigates and two sloops of war and seventy-five cargo ships. Wind was light. Westerly and then from the south. But mostly westerly."

"You saw them sail?" asked Rougecroix.

Gubu, with a blunt forefinger on which the nail had been reduced to a little diamond of horn, ruffled the feathers on the back of the parrot's neck.

"I did," he said.

"How did you get here so fast then, with the same light wind?" asked Rougecroix. ·

"I used the sweeps," said Gubu. Rougecroix reflected on this. It was possible. Gubu commanded nothing more than a thirty-foot inter-island trading sloop. In light wind it could outsail the vessels of the convoy readily. In no wind it could make three knots, using the long oars called sweeps.

Having got his hundred francs and the blue-and-yellow parrot as well, Gubu left. His sloop was anchored outside the bay, and he had been rowed to *Bonne Chance* in a little two-man dinghy whose weathered sides were almost void of paint. There were two oarsmen in the dinghy, both blacks, and they grinned at the sight of the parrot.

"I'm coming on board," yelled Gubu at them angrily.

"Yes, sir," they said. Then one of them recollected himself and, fishing inside his blouse, took out a whistle on which he blew a wavering note. When this was done, Gubu lowered himself down the chain plates into the dinghy bobbing below and set off for his little sloop, the big parrot still on his wrist. Rougecroix, looking after him through the lantern lights of his cabin, said, "He's so stupid, some day he'll hang."

Toward evening of the same day, the frigate *Leopard* worked her way ahead of the convoy into the Windward Passage and, keeping over on the Haiti side, started to crawl up that dangerous strip of water in the ghost of a westerly. There was a heavy slop in the channel which threw her about, and her guns bucked and strained at their lashings. Her yards, on which stunsails were set to catch even the promise of a wind, banged against their housings, and her sails flapped and snapped in the air currents caused by her pitching masts.

The heat was cruel on deck and intolerable on the gun decks. Wallowing in the slop, *Leopard* dipped her gunports occasionally, so these had been shut lest the charges (already in the guns) should become damp.

Manly Treegate, confined to the gun deck with his crew for the time being, had been almost three months now in His Majesty's service. His fair hair, once tied loosely in a blue ribbon, was now wrapped in a piece of tarred cloth, forming a stiff queue or pigtail on the back of his neck. There were a number of bruises, some old and some new, on his back, most of them the work of Midshipman Prynne. He was no longer well fleshed out but gaunt, and there was at times, when he thought of Midshipman Prynne, a look in his eyes of cold hate. He could have saved himself a quantity of blows if he could have learned to flinch and whine a little in the presence of the midshipman. But this, although advised to do it by his gun-captain, who had befriended him in his first encounter with Prynne, he would not do.

"It may take a year or two years," said Weeks, "but he'll beat and haze you until you flinch and whine a bit."

"It will take longer than that," said Manly. "I don't come of a family of whiners."

*Leopard*'s job, getting into the Passage ahead of the convoy, was to see if it was clear of shipping—not merely French ships-of-war like the mysterious two-decker that had mauled her two months back and was suspected to be still about, but even fishing boats and inter-island luggers. With wind, the task would have been easy, but without wind, *Leopard,* sighting a strange sail, had to lower a boat and investigate. Having only three boats, she could not investigate every sail she saw, and so, as she got into the Passage and started working her way up it, she didn't send a boat to question a thirty-foot trading sloop captained by a tall black wearing a tattered French officer's coat. Perhaps she would have done so, but at that moment there was a welcome stiffening of the westerly into a ten-knot breeze, and rather than miss this wind, the frigate ignored the sloop and plunged on, and the sloop passed, headed south.

Manly hadn't seen the sloop, but since the westerly held and the guns did not need watching, the men were allowed up on the spar deck. He climbed into the rigging to cool off and noted the distant mountains of Cuba and the much closer mountains of Haiti and tried to calculate the distance to land. He reckoned between seven and eight miles to Haiti. The current, however, set offshore, and he would not be able to swim that distance against the current. The soft mountains of Haiti rose emerald and gold out of the brilliant blue sea and, soaring skyward,

119

were swathed here and there in snatches of silver cloud. The clouds threw cool blue-black shadows over the mountain ridges and valleys, and just the sight of all that loveliness filled Manly with infinite longing to plunge into the azure sea and try to make it ashore.

Weeks warned him not to try. Anyone who went over the side to swim ashore, if not picked up by a boat, became a mark for the marines, who would open fire on him. True, they might not kill him. But they were almost sure to wound him. And then would come the sharks. Weeks said that at Trafalgar the sharks had been so thick you could almost walk on them.

"They come when they hear guns," he explained. "They know when they're going to feed."

But still Manly looked longingly at the land and thought of escape. He was determined to try if he had as much as half a chance. This might be his last sight of land for weeks, he realized, and with the shoreline so close, he made up his mind that sometime that night he would make his attempt.

120

# 13

THE mild westerly which had filled *Leopard*'s sails when she sighted the little sloop lasted for just over an hour, so that the frigate was able to get well ino the Passage before it died. The same wind did not reach the first vessels of the convoy until twenty minutes later. *Leopard,* at sunset, was eight miles ahead of her charges and the wind coming in from the south with the setting of the sun. Sir Thomas Carroll on *Leopard* shortened sail to close the gap between him and the vessels he was to protect.

Sir Thomas knew that the French privateer *Bonne Chance* was about. She was notorious in the islands and would not miss an opportunity such as that offered by the convoy. He was worried about her slipping out of one of the Haitian bays and cutting off a straggler. But he was more concerned about that mysterious French two-decker which had mauled him two months previously. She was now known to be *Indomptable,* which had escaped the Mediterranean blockage in a gale some months earlier. If she got in among the merchantmen, armed though they were, she would be like a hound among rabbits. It was comforting to see *Centurion*'s old-fashioned, long-cut top-sails to the south, as the sun slid westward over the distant peaks of Cuba and darkness fell. She was where she ought to be, and more than a match for the French two-decker.

The convoy had been ordered to show no lights while in the Passage except one white light on the stern. The ships were to close up with the setting of the sun and set double watches, and Sir Thomas saw them start huddling closer, like sheep expecting a long night and a cold wind.

For one moment, as the sun slid to the horizon, the whole mass of Cuba stood out bold and sharp against the sky, caught between night and day. Then the sun was gone in a furnace of red, orange and saffron, and over Haiti to the east Venus glimmered, liquid in the dying sky.

At *Leopard*'s foretop, where he had been sent as look-out, Manly Treegate watched with sinking heart the dark bulk of Haiti slowly change its shape and position to the eastward. He hadn't reckoned on the wind hold-ing, and once they were clear of the last peninsula of the island, his chances of escape were nil. Ahead lay the open ocean, and beyond that England and months, perhaps years, of blockade duty off some freezing European port. Prynne had sent him aloft, probably suspecting that he might slip over the side and swim for the shore as soon as it was dark. There was no chance whatever of gaining the deck now. He would have to wait until relieved.

A dark blob appeared some distance off in the water—a shapeless thing which puzzled Manly until he decided it was the island of Tortuga. Between it and the vast bulk of Haiti the ocean was barely visible. Manly's attention was drawn after a while to a tiny spot close to the western end of Tortuga. He thought it but a rock which showed a touch of white from waves cresting over it. Then he saw it was moving, so it was a vessel coming out from the western end of Tortuga and headed toward the convoy on a beam reach.

The marine who was on lookout with him was facing in the other direction and, judging from the depth and regularity of his breathing, was asleep. Manly turned again to the vessel and thought he could make out top-sails on the foremast, though the sails were mere geo-metrical shapes or suggestions of shapes in the obscurity of the night.

*Bonne Chance?* He had been told to look out for the privateer. She was faster than any of His Majesty's frig-ates except in a gale or wind, and although not a match for them in armament, she carried eighteen-pounders. But why would *Bonne Chance* set out to fight a frigate for whom she was no match? He should give the alarm but decided not to. He owed no loyalty to the frigate and her brutal officers, and so continued to watch the scarcely discernible sail but said nothing. Whatever she was up to, he would help her by delaying giving the alarm until the last moment. The schooner tacked and her shape was swallowed in the dark bulk of Tortuga for several minutes. When she reappeared, it was in the strip of water between Tortuga and Haiti, and she was much nearer—so much so that Manly could delay reporting her no longer.

"Sail broad on the starboard beam," he shouted, and the lookout on the main, who had been dozing, immediately confirmed the report. There was a scurrying on the deck, and three lighted lanterns were sent whirling aloft on the upper topgallant yard. But the strange sail made no reply. Instead, there was a sudden blinding explosion of light in the darkness, followed by a thundering roar which echoed among the mountains of the vast island, and a swarm of round shot plopped into the water around *Leopard*—one cutting the outer jibstay two feet from the foremast.

Then the clacking of rattles and the roll of drums broke out on the deck and Manly slid down to the deck and dashed to the power room for cartridges and quills.

The guns were already loaded and run out and awaiting the order to fire. But this did not come immediately. The privateer, having fired herself, had turned neatly on her heels and darted back into the obscurity of Tortuga. There was no target.

Midshipman Prynne at his station behind the guns spotted Manly. "Treegate," he said, "you'll get a dozen of the best for this. Asleep on the foretop. You should have reported that vessel sooner. I'll see that Grogham lays them on." Grogham was the bosun's mate with the strongest arm. Manly said nothing.

"Silence on the gun deck," yelled Marston, the gunnery officer, and, "Mr. Prynne, are your guns ready?"

"Yes, sir," said Prynne.

"Then raise your moldy hand, you useless cub! If we have a misfire, I'll masthead you." Weeks was standing by the breech of the gun, the glowing slow match in his hand, ready to put it to the quill in the touchhole. The lanterns swung from their hooks overhead, each casting its pool of light over the gun and the crew below, and the faces of the men were caught in the changing play of glow and shadow.

Nothing could be seen through the gunport but a square patch of dark sea with the sky above it, but the crew could feel the frigate heel slightly as she went over to the starboard tack to run down on Tortuga, in whose shadow the privateer was hiding. Then from the deck there came a series of sharp commands and they knew the privateer had at last been sighted. Weeks blew on the end of the slow match and the spark glowed and shed a ruddy light over his cheeks and the end of his nose.

"Starboard broadside, fire," cried Marston, and Weeks put the match to the quill. In an instant the gun and those on either side jerked back against their breechings, and a choking, acrid cloud of battle smoke swept through the ports. The swabber already had his ramrod down the barrel, Manly passed him a cartridge and gave a new quill to Weeks, and the gun was reloaded and run out even before the smoke had cleared away. Another broadside followed and then a third—all delivered by the starboard battery—so it was plain that the chase was close by, though nobody on the gun deck could see her. In passing a cartridge, Manly got a quick look through the gunport and discovered that they were almost clear of Tortuga, having chased the privateer up the channel between it and Haiti. No answering fire could be heard on the gun deck, and Redding, who as a volunteer was allowed one or two minor privileges, asked Marston whether the fire was successful.

"Don't know," he said. "Don't see her. She's somewhere between us and Haiti and only visible from the tops." She would be visible from the tops, Manly reflected. If one looked down at her, she would show up against the sea, which was lighter than the land. But it was an odd kind of battle—three broadsides fired at an unseen target. And what was the privateer doing attacking a frigate, in any case?

The answer came in a shattering roar from the other side of the ship. A gun burst from its breechings, jumped off its carriage and lumbered across the deck, killing two men. Pieces of wood hummed like angry wasps through the air. Lanterns fell from their hooks and spilled their oil over the gun deck. A fire started immediately, lighting up the whole place in a pleasant yellow glow. Manly saw a man staring in disbelief at the scarlet stump of his arm and another lying motionless in a growing pool of blood only a few feet from him. Passing a cartridge to the swabber, he looked for Prynne and did not see him, but guessed what had happened.

The trap was sprung. The privateer had lured *Leopard* into the gap between the two islands, and the two-decker

*Indomptable,* lying in the shadow off Tortuga, had emerged and fired a broadside into the frigate, delivered from only half a mile off. She was caught between the privateer on one side and the two-decker on the other. *Centurion,* ten miles off and making scarcely two knots in a light wind, could do nothing to help her.

# 14

For the next twenty minutes *Leopard* endured the pounding of *Indomptable* and *Bonne Chance* and spat back her defiance of them. The wind hardly filled her shot-ridden sails and was not enough to move away the choking clouds of gun smoke which surrounded her. Manly, sweating in the heat of the gun deck, choked and coughed at his work, his eyes streaming tears, his lungs seared by smoke and fumes.

*Indomptable* and *Bonne Chance* pounded away at *Leopard,* firing at her gun flashes, which were seen as orange blooms through the heavy smoke. On Manly's side—the starboard battery—*Bonne Chance*'s long eighteen-pounders were firing high at the rigging, so *Leopard*'s gun deck did not suffer as heavily here. But on the larboard side, where *Indomptable* was firing with her twenty-four-pounders, the damage was horrible. Lifting the hatch amidships to go down to the powder hold for more cartridges, Manly hesitated a moment to look at the larboard battery. The flash of a broadside lit the scene for a moment and he saw three guns in a row silent, with their crews dead around them. The whole side of the ship between two of the gunports had been blown away, and one of the guns swung around, its breeching burst, and pointed along the length of the frigate. A party of marines at that moment thrust through the swirl of gunsmoke, pitching the dead and wounded out of the exploded area between the two gunports. They lifted up a dead man in the lurid battle glow and Manly, with a wrench at his heart, recognized the thin face of Coffin. Coffin should not have been on the gun deck, but had seemingly been sent down to replace men already killed. Since boarding *Leopard* together, Manly had had only glimpses of Coffin, who was one of the upper-deck crew, and had been unable to say a word to him. Now he was dead. Sick at the thought, Manly ducked down the hatch and along the utterly dark companionway, which led to another hatch beyond curtains of heavy canvas, and this directly to the powder hold.

Down here, the confusion was suddenly quelled, for the felt-padded walls admitted no noise. The lantern behind its pane of glass burned serenely, like a votive light in a church, and despite the tubs of powder around and the stacks of cartridges and lengths of fuses, the powder hold seemed the safest place on board. He filled his bucket with cartridges, and Roberts, the boy from Redding's gun, came in. His face was black with powder smoke.

"Seen Prynne?" asked Roberts fiercely.

"No," said Manly. Prynne, he recalled, was no longer behind his gun.

"He's hiding," said Roberts savagely. "He always does. If I see him, I'll kill him." He was gone immediately with his bucket of cartridges. Manly followed him out. As he closed the hatch, he saw a movement in the shadowy area away from the lamp and Prynne's frightened face showed for a moment. Disgusted, Manly shut the hatch. When he gained the gun deck, Marston was standing by the hatchway and yelled to him to go to the larboard side. He found his own crew had been transferred there, but the smoke was beginning to clear away from the area. A heavy silence had descended suddenly on the gun deck, and through the smoke he could see men lying about the deck in horrid pools and several guns tumbled off their carriages. Glancing through the smashed sides of the frigate, Manly saw *Indomptable* a hundred yards off sailing toward the convoy, having partly disabled *Leopard*. Suddenly Prynne was there, his face rather clean in the light of the lantern, but his white stockings and breeches splattered with blood.

"Clear these decks," he said. "Get these men overboard." Everybody stared at him for a moment and then, knowing Prynne, hurried to obey. Weeks picked up a man who was plainly dead and tumbled him through the breach over the side. Three more, lifeless, were tumbled after him, but the gunners hesitated over the wounded. The sharks were thick around the frigate.

"Over with them," cried Prynne. "I want these decks cleared," he piped. One of the wounded men, propped against a smashed bulkhead, lifted his head and said, "Leave me a while. It won't be long."

"Perdition," cried Prynne, white with rage at not being instantly obeyed. "Get these men overboard." He seized the wounded man who had spoken by the shoulders as if personally to throw him over the side. A dark wave of anger surged up in Manly, but it was Redding who exploded.

"Leave that man be, Mr. Prynne," he said in a voice so sharp that Prynne whirled around on him, amazed.

"You mutinous swine . . ." piped Prynne, and then something in Redding's face cut off whatever he was going to say and he stopped short.

"You're a stinking little coward," Redding said. "You're a disgrace to your ship and your uniform and I've half a mind to fling you to the sharks myself." He reached out to grab Prynne but was seized in a moment by his own shipmates. They would have let him go, but a corporal of marines seized him and, calling for help, had in a moment tied his hands behind him. The cockpit was full of wounded—for not all the officers jettisoned wounded men, there being a shortage of hands—and Prynne, who had recovered himself, ordered Redding tied to a ringbolt on the deck and a marine sentry placed over him as guard.

"You'll smart for this in the morning," he said. "I'll have the hide off of you." He got black looks from the crew, but they were powerless to help the volunteer.

*Leopard* had thirty-five dead and sixty wounded, which was reckoned a moderate loss, the ship having had to endure for twenty minutes the broadside of two vessels. She had been holed several times below the waterline, but her pumps were just able, in the quiet sea, to keep up with the leaks. The carpenter was busy below deck, moving her stores to find the shot holes. The frigate's main damage was to her masts. She had lost her foremast and bowsprit and half the main. The bosun was occupied in jury-rigging a foremast and bowsprit, for without some sail up forward, her helm was useless. Had the wind been anything but light, she would have been driven up on the coast of Haiti or of Tortuga and wrecked. As it was, she had turned around in the water to face into the southerly breeze and kept coming up into it and then falling back in a series of erratic staggers that made the work aboard all the more difficult. It was an hour before the bosun could get a makeshift spritsail yard rigged on the stump of the bowsprit to give the helmsman some control. Meanwhile, in the dark of the night, blossoms of flames flourished in the convoy as *Indomptable* did her work among the merchantmen.

A fingernail of moon showed low in the sky and gave enough light to show three of the convoy being hustled away toward Haiti. *Bonne Chance,* like a wolf among sheep, was running her victims off to their doom. Now, Manly knew, was his chance to escape if he was ever going to have one. The side of the gun deck was laid open for fifteen feet by *Indomptable*'s broadsides, and he had only to slip through and into the water to be clear of the frigate. Everything was in a state of confusion and no one was likely to see him. Even if he was seen, the work of saving the frigate would hardly be stopped to bring him back aboard. But he was afraid of the sharks. Weeks had said they were always thick about ships in time of battle and there must be many of them about. He stole to the frigate's side to take a look and was peering down into the murk of the water when a rope's end was brought sharply down across his shoulders.

"Lazy dog," cried Prynne. "Back to your work." And he raised his arm to bring the rope down again. But Manly had now been driven beyond endurance. The sight of the bloodied deck, the memory of the dead and dying men tumbled over the side, and the memory of Prynne, cowering in the powder hold, was too much for him. He seized Prynne's arm with one hand and struck the midshipman full in the face with the other. Prynne staggered back and Manly was on him in a moment and bore him to the ground. Prynne somehow got himself free and stood for a moment, yelling for help by the shattered bulkhead. But, before anybody could interfere, Manly flung himself at Prynne again, and Prynne, reaching backward, grabbed Manly so that the two of them went over the side and plunged with a splash into the water.

Manly surfaced first. The frigate was already drawing away. Prynne seized him from behind and forced his head under the water, not in fight but in panic, trying to save himself. Manly went under readily without resisting, and Prynne let go. Then Manly surfaced again, some distance off. There was a swift movement in the water beside him, and he reached for his sheath knife.

The sharks were thick about, as Weeks had said.

# 15

GUBU, in his little thirty-foot, fat-bellied trading sloop, had been dismayed to see *Leopard* coming up the Windward Passage in light airs. He knew she was on her way with the convoy, but he had not expected her so soon, and seeing her enter the passage just as he had been about to quit the southern end, he thought he would be taken. But the frigate, instead of sending a boat over, had caught the wind at that moment after a horrible hour of slopping in the entrance to the channel, and so he was saved. He cleared the entrance to the Passage and then turned east along the south coast of Haiti to a little bay guarded by a reef and hidden behind the shoulder of a mountain. There he dropped anchor and called his crew, which consisted of the two men who had rowed him over to *Bonne Chance* and an old black crone woman called Mama Amelie, who could cook and bear a hand at the tiller too. She was also a witch doctor in the kind of witchcraft which was called "obiah." She smoked a short clay pipe, black with nicotine and tar, and she had two thumbs on her right hand—a big one and a little one growing out of it—which was the certain sign of an "obiah woman."

"We got cash," said Gubu when his crew had gathered aft on the deck with him. "And we got this parrot. The parrot's mine."

Mama Amelie eyed the bird from behind her withered lids and the parrot turned its head to one side, closed one eye and stared back at her out of the other.

"That bird's mean," she said. "Lot of folks gonna die." The other two looked uneasily at each other. Mama Amelie's prophecies were horrible because they always came true, though rarely as expected.

"Better get rid of that bird, Cap," said one.

"No," said Gubu. "That's the prettiest thing I ever did have in my life. I'm keeping that bird. Ain't nobody gonna touch that bird."

"What you gonna call her?" asked Mama Amelie.

"Jezebel," said Gubu. And that was settled.

Gubu now took out the money he had received from Rougecroix. He divided it carefully into five equal parts—a share for himself and each of the crew and one for the ship. He was going to give a share to Jezebel, but there was too much grumbling, so he didn't. When the division was done, he went to his little cabin, opened a strongbox, into which he put his own share of the money, and took out a stone jug of white French rum. Mama Amelie brought a pannikin and he poured her a generous measure, which she sucked down, her thin throat working like the neck of a tortoise. The rum tasted harsh, but in a little while they were all smiling and Gubu was humming a song in patois of which most of the words were gibberish. It had been, originally, a folk tune from the South of France called "Mes Moutons."

The pannikin had gone around three times when Gubu had the great idea which would make them all rich. It wasn't an original idea but merely the decision that he himself apply the hundred-year-old strategy of the buccaneers. A big merchant fleet was at the moment making its way up the Windward Passage nearby. It was getting dark and the ships guarding the fleet would be dispersed. Why not slip in among the merchantmen in his little sloop, which could certainly arouse no suspicion, pick some vessel which had drifted away from the body of the convoy, board and take her? The reward would certainly be greater than the hundred francs he had just divided among his crew.

He explained his plan to his crew with a great deal of gesticulation, for the rum was going to his head, and they argued and shouted so, that it looked as if they would come to blows. Then they agreed, and Gubu solemnly picked up the crock of white rum and locked it away—the first essential of the venture.

With the coming of the night, a land breeze established itself around the coastline of Haiti. The air on the mountaintops grew colder and heavier and slid down their sides, displacing the warmer air below which was forced to move seaward. The little tubby sloop had the benefit of this breeze, for she hugged the coastline, but the convoy, farther out to sea, felt only little puffs from it. The sloop sped out of its cozy bay on this land breeze, with Gubu at the tiller, at his feet a pile of cutlasses and pistols comprising the ship's arms chest.

She cleared the reef and in a little while had turned the corner of the southern coast of Haiti and was in the Windward Passage. Over the dark and invisible sea a host of tiny golden stars hovered like fireflies—the stern lights of the ships of the convoy. They were huddled together in the center of the channel and so could not get the benefit of the shore breeze. Gubu handed the tiller to one of his crew and went forward to look for a likely victim. He needed a solitary, smallish ship near the Haiti shore but still not within the orbit of the wind. But a solitary vessel was not to be seen. The cloud of golden stars hung together in mid-channel, crawling northward. An hour went by with not a prize offering, and then another. The rum began to wear off and Gubu began to wonder whether his plan was wise. Then to the north of him there was a sudden bright flash and the thunder of guns. His crew was immediately panicked. The man at the tiller, without any order, tacked the sloop and flung her about to head out of the channel and back to the safety of the little bay as fast as possible.

Gubu snatched the tiller away and put the sloop back on her course. They yelled at each other, while over the sea a terrible silence descended. And then there came again the shattering explosion of a broadside, this time on a deeper note. *"Indomptable,"* said Gubu and grinned.

Though the others might quail, he knew this was his chance. The merchantmen would scatter, hampered by light air in getting away from the gunfire, and surely one of them must come his way. In a little while his patience was rewarded. The firing continued and increased in intensity, and a small brig of perhaps no more than a hundred tons detached itself from the convoy and started to move toward the Haiti coast. Gubu glanced about and realized that against the dense mass of Haiti he was invisible from seaward. He watched the brig and spilled the wind from his sails to slow the sloop in the water. In five minutes, with all aboard the brig occupied with the battle to the north, he had nursed the sloop to within pistol shot of her. A few moments later the sloop slid against the brig's foremast chain plates. She had now been seen at the last moment and someone hailed her from the brig's deck with an oath, seeing a collision imminent and not suspecting the sloop's mission. Then Gubu and his men fumbled aboard, up the chain plates, cutlasses dangling from lanyards about their necks or held in their teeth, and they fell on the unsuspecting crew.

They almost lost the battle. The crew fled under the initial assault and Gubu suddenly remembered the sloop and Jezebel. He wondered if anybody had tied the sloop to the brig, and turned to investigate. He found the sloop drifting away from the side of the brig. Instead of leading his men, he jumped back on board and his little crew were left alone. Dismayed at seeing him go, they rushed for the chain plates themselves. But Mama Amelie's blood was up. She slapped one of them across the face with the flat of a cutlass and then fired a pistol directly into the knot of sailors bunched for a counterattack. Screaming like a wildcat, she charged at the seamen and they dispersed. Gubu climbed back on board, the other two rallied, and the brig was taken—very largely by Mama Amelie. The brig would not have fallen so readily but that it was seriously undermanned, a number of her crew having been taken off to bring the British warships up to strength. Also, her captain had been incautious enough to go to her topmast with the only other ship's officer to see what the firing was about. So there was no one to direct her defense, and her men were not armed. In the brief assault, one of the brig's crew had been killed and two were lightly wounded. Gubu's crew had suffered nothing, and the brig, laden with sugar and Grenada spices, proved a very rich prize indeed.

The sloop was now tied to the brig's stern, so Gubu's mind was easy about her. He sent one of the hands back to her, largely to keep Jezebel company so she wouldn't fly away, and he turned to the problem of securing the brig. Her crew were all put below and the hatch locked on them, but the captain and her first officer were locked in the captain's cabin. Gubu left them there to be dealt with later. The battle was dying away to the north of him and he was much nearer the northern than the southern coast of Haiti. His cozy little bay lay on the south coast, but it was a trifle too small to take the brig into. Furthermore, the breeze had died and the wind turned southerly, so he could not beat his way back to it. His best plan, he decided, was to work his way close to the Haiti shore, slip around the north coast and put in at Port-au-Paix, where he could sell the brig's cargo. He took the wheel himself and coaxed the brig, whose stern light he had extinguished, closer to the Haiti shore. He hoped for a ghost of the land breeze. What he got was a series of weak puffs coming down the valleys between the peaks. But these, with the light southerly, gave him more speed than the rest of the convoy, from which he drew farther and farther away.

The battle to the north had now died away altogether, though he could not see any of the vessels taking part. Then there was a heavy explosion three miles away and a pillar of flame and smoke rose into the night sky, lighting the shipping around. Soon another ship was afire and then another, and from this Gubu guessed that *Indomptable* had gotten into the merchant fleet. He continued to nurse his prize northward, very pleased with his night's work.

Manly Treegate swam for a long time, his nerves on edge and his sheath knife in his hand, in the warm Caribbean Sea. Time and again, hearing a swirling in the water about him, he expected a shark to attack, but nothing happened. There were plenty about, he knew. He could see the white streak of phosphorescence they made in the water, but either they did not find him or they sensed he might be dangerous and left him for easier prey. He hoped he was headed for the Haiti shore, but he was actually swimming in a circle, for he came at last to a ten-foot section of *Leopard*'s broken bowsprit which the bosun and his riggers had thrown over the side. It floated in billows of the outer jib, which had been thrown overboard with it, and there was a tangle of sheets and shrouds around it. The frigate had gone off in the dark. Manly climbed into the billows of the sail and then got astride the bowsprit with just his legs in the water. Immersed in the folds of the sail, his legs might be protected from the sharks.

Of Prynne he had seen nothing and he cared nothing. Haiti he estimated was about five miles off, and when daylight came and he was rested, he should be able to get to it. His world was now reduced to the few feet of visibility along the spar and the sail. Westward he saw the merchant ships burning, and he hoped that daylight might reveal a waterlogged boat or two floating around. His mind was heavy and demanded sleep, but he forced it to work, and after a weary wrestle with possibilities and probabilities, he decided that he could do nothing until daylight and he had better rest now, for he must work then. He leaned forward on the spar, laid his head on a mound of sopping sail and was instantly asleep.

An hour later he was awake with an uneasy feeling of imminent danger. It was still dark, but the southerly wind had a touch of west in it and was blowing stronger. He thought it was the wind that had wakened him, until he heard a splashing sound to the south of him. Out of the darkness came a vast shape which for a panicked moment he believed was a whale and then recognized as the bow of a ship. It was headed straight for him and would run over him and the spar in a moment. He saw the flash of white from under the forefoot, reached up and jumped as best he could. One hand caught a shroud, and flailing with his feet, he found the rigging of the dolphin striker. He hauled himself, with great pains, up to the bowsprit, and, stooping, ran along this onto the deck. Then in the light of a lantern hidden behind the gunwale he saw a black crone coming toward him. She wore a blood-stained rag of a dress and had a cutlass almost as big as herself hanging from her neck by a lanyard.

"Eh, eh, Gubu," cried Mama Amelie. "You got a parrot, but I got me a pretty boy right out of the sea."

# 16

GUBU wanted to put Manly down the forehatch with the captured crew of the brig, but Mama Amelie would not allow this. She looked closely at the boy in the light of the lantern, making little clucking noises with her tongue. He had blue eyes and golden hair (though gathered together at the back in a tarred rag). His skin, sunburned as it was, was much fairer than she was accustomed to seeing, and she was quite taken with it. She noted a number of welts on his torso, made by ropes, and she knew what they meant. So she told Gubu that the boy was hers and no one was to harm him.

Gubu didn't like the decision. But he did not dare run counter to Mama Amelie, who certainly had powers that had to be respected. She could make a man fall sick just by looking at him. He agreed that Manly was not to be locked below, but if he got them into trouble, Mama

Amelie would be responsible. Then he glowered at Manly and went off muttering while Mama Amelie, deciding that the boy was hungry, got him something to eat. The brig had a great store of fresh fruit, having left Jamaica only the day before. Mama Amelie brought Manly bananas, oranges and guavas and told him to eat his fill.

The very sight of the fruit made his mouth water and the taste was almost too much for him. He bit into an orange, and a flood of pain dispersed through the muscles of his jaws. He almost cried out and, putting the orange aside, tried a banana, which he found he could manage. But the change of diet, from salt horse and ship's biscuit to fresh tropical fruit, caused almost as much pain as pleasure and he ate only little.

*"T'as peur?"* asked Mama Amelie, seeing his appetite so small. Manly had had two years of Fench instruction from a French governess before his father died, but she had to repeat the question before he realized that she was asking him if he was afraid. He said he wasn't, and this was true. He was merely tired. When he had eaten the banana, all his thoughts seemed to go from him. Whatever kind of ship he was on, he was safe for the present. His eyes closed, though he struggled to keep them open, and he fell asleep on the deck. Clucking to herself, Mama Amelie went off to find something to cover him from the spray.

Gubu was delighted with the brig. She had a figurehead of a woman carrying a shell in her hands, and her name, he discovered from the captain (for he could not read), was *Constance*. She had a heavy mount of guns—

four eight-pounder carronades aft (two to a side); eight long nine-pounders amidships; and a long eighteen-pounder forward of her foremast. This last was mounted on a wheel or swivel so that it could be fired to larboard or starboard. Neither Gubu nor the two men who formed his crew knew how to load them, and they were in fact afraid of them. But they pretended to fire them, going "boom" to each other as they put an imaginary slow match to the touchhole.

The next morning Gubu got rid of the captain and his officer by putting them over the side in a boat. He told the crew that they could take a choice of going with their captain or staying with him. They had been recruited in Kingston, Jamaica, a city which together with Port Royal (now destroyed) had long been the haunt of pirates. They all agreed to sail with Gubu, for as merchant seamen they could look for only miserable rewards sailing, but "on the account" a coach-and-four was not beyond their grasp.

Gubu now had a full crew for the brig and the little sloop. He put some of the brig's crew on the sloop with instructions to rendezvous with him at Port-au-Paix. Manly, having slept all through the night, woke refreshed about midmorning and began to find out something about the kind of ship he was on. The crew, being Jamaicans, spoke a lazy kind of English and used the old-style pronouns "thee" and "thou" profusely. He was amazed to learn that the brig had been taken by the tiny sloop that now bobbed astern of them, and it was plain from this that the big black, Gubu, was either a pirate or a privateer. The difference between the two was a matter of great importance, Manly well knew.

A privateer, sailing under authority of a government, could attack and take "enemy vessels," though sometimes the definition of "enemy" was stretched to extend to neutrals. If taken himself, a privateer had to be treated as a prisoner of war. A pirate sailed "on his own account," without authority from any government. He attacked any vessel he thought he could capture. And if he were captured himself, he was hanged. The difference between a privateer and a pirate was in essence the difference between life and death. Mama Amelie brought Manly a pannikin of turtle stew (there were six fresh turtles aboard in a pen amidships), and he asked her whether Gubu was a privateer. She didn't know what the word meant. He tried to explain but she couldn't understand. She brought Gubu to him and Gubu could not understand either. But he caught the word *"drapeau"* for flag and he understood that. He sent one of the hands to rummage through the flag locker, and not finding there what was required, he cut a square of black tarpaulin out of an old boat cover and sent this aloft—the ragged black flag of piracy. He was delighted with it and called all hands and made them cheer it. They seemed quite happy too.

For Manly this meant that he had exchanged imprisonment on a British frigate for service on a Haitian pirate. He had gone from the frying pan, it seemed, into the fire.

Toward midday the wind, which had been light all

morning, came up briskly from the west and the brig bowled along happily before it. She was a smart sailor, passing cleanly through the water, and running before the wind, she was soon making eight knots. The bow wave at her forefoot was dazzling white in the brilliant sun, and aft the blue water bubbled in a flat trail from her transom. This, for a brig, was the easiest point of sailing— making for the least work at the wheel—and there was a holiday air aboard. Everybody looked forward to reaching Port-au-Paix, where Gubu would certainly celebrate his fine capture with generosity.

There was a lookout in the foretop, but the hands were taking ease about the decks, a number of them playing a gambling game with a small top called "Crown and Anchor." Mama Amelie had resumed her principal duties, which were those of cook, and she gave plenty of food, highly spiced, to Manly, who devoured it, for it seemed to him impossible to get enough to eat.

He made a few cautious inquiries among the English-speaking Jamaicans about the port to which they were headed, but only two of them had ever been to it and that on French ships some years before. The country about, they said, was "wild." There were no roads into the interior and all traffic around the whole island was carried on by sea. This, Manly reasoned, would mean that there would be a number of sailing craft calling at Port-au-Paix and he could hope to slip aboard one of them bound for a French island closer to America.

They reached Port-au-Paix in midafternoon, with the little sloop arriving some hours later. Gubu, dressed in his

Chausseur's coat and with his blue-and-gold parrot on his shoulder, was rowed immediately ashore to look to the sale of the cargo. Another boat went ashore a little after, and Manly contrived to get into it by going forward to the bow, where he was least likely to be seen. The boat got away before Mama Amelie found he was gone. As soon as it touched the dock, Manly darted down one of the streets leading to the center of the town and was lost in the crowd.

The streets were crowded with blacks and mulattoes in ragged clothing, all barefooted, some with terrible sores on their feet and legs, and the men all wearing hats made of palm fronds, the women wearing a kind of turban of colored cloth. The houses were of mud, with palm-frond thatch which was thick with insects. Rust-colored cockroaches scurried about the thatch, falling occasionally to the ground or on the people passing below. A centipede a foot long was pushing its way into a crack in a wall as Manly passed by, and clouds of flies arose from the pools of water which lay in the middle of all the streets.

The poverty and squalor of the town were horrifying. He found a little girl sitting by the side of a house, too sick to brush the flies off her face, and he passed several people whose limbs were swollen by elephantiasis, which was called "big foot." For all their poverty and sickness, however, the mass of people made a great deal of noise, shouting to each other and laughing with a screech not unlike that of a parrot. There was a square at the landward end of the town, in the center of which stood a church surrounded by a graveyard that was overgrown with weeds and bushes. The church was in ruins, but it seemed to offer, in all the noise and heat, a place to rest and think.

Manly went inside through a door that had parted company with the upper hinge, and a rat the size of a small dog scurried off in the gloom. A shaft of sunlight struck through a ruined window against a moldering wall, and in the bright patch it made, a snuff-colored lizard basked.

Manly entered cautiously, his footsteps muffled on the dusty floor of packed clay. As his eyes grew accustomed to the gloom, he saw what had been the altar, now reduced to a pile of rubble. The niches which had once housed statues in the adobe walls were black with cobwebs. Only a few pews remained, and these were broken and had been flung across each other like jackstraws. A fire had been lit before the altar and a quantity of paper and clothing burned on it. Manly picked up what remained of a charred prayer book but flung it hastily from him when he found the underside was crawling with pale grey insects. The church, he assumed, had been ruined in the slave revolt of some years before, and plainly nobody now visited it. It offered, he thought, a good place to hide—a shelter until Gubu had sailed with his brig and Manly could look about for a vessel bound for a French island. He would be safer on a French island because France was at war with Britain and the French might respect his claim to American citizenship and help him to get back to America. His immediate problem was to avoid recapture by Gubu, and he decided he would remain in the ruined church until dusk and then he would forage for food. He wasn't likely to go hungry, he decided. In the squalid town he had seen an abundance of fruit trees, many of them neglected but bearing. He might go short of meat and of bread, but he would find enough fruit to keep him alive. His head felt a little hot, and the world still had a tendency to spin and sideslip about him because of his months at sea. He sat down by the door of the church, where he could keep an eye on anyone approaching, and watched the shadows lengthen among the weeds and tangled vines in the graveyard outside.

After a while there were some scurryings in the shadows of the ruined church and he remembered the rat as big as a dog. As the darkness grew and the rats became bolder, the temptation to quit the church and take his chances on the brig became stronger, but he resisted it. He was far better off where he was, he decided, than at sea on a pirate ship, facing the certainty of being hanged if captured.

# 17

MANLY had a night of horror in the old church. The huge rats—they were called "agouti," he learned later—spent the hours of darkness hunting food and fighting among themselves. Twice during the night when he had fallen into a heavy doze he was wakened by them sniffing at his clothing. Also, there were a number of bats, far larger than those that appeared in the summer evenings in Salem, flitting about the church and giving little cat cries. Then toward dawn he began to feel cramps in his stomach, followed by spasms of retching. When daylight came, the stomach cramps were worse and the retching almost continuous. The change of diet—from salt beef and dry biscuit on *Leopard* to the rich turtle meat and vegetables and fruits he had received from Mama Amelie and of which he had eaten plenteously—was too much for his constitution.

He spent the day in misery, eating and drinking nothing through the long hot hours, too weak to move, and then he endured another nightmare night among the fighting rats. By the following day he had a fever. He tried to get out of the church, which had become a place of horror for him, and managed to totter a few feet into the shambles of the graveyard which surrounded it. Here he propped himself up against an old tombstone on which a death's head was significantly carved, and he endured the terrible heat of the tropical sun rather than go back into the church again among the rats. How long he remained propped against the gravestone he did not know. Between fever and dysentery, he had had only a few snatches of consciousness, and even these merged with the fantasies that flooded through his brain. He saw a brilliant black-and-yellow bird sitting on a bush covered with red trumpet-shaped flowers, and he knew this was real because beyond it was the crumbling adobe wall of the church. Then he was on the gun deck of *Leopard,* the thunder of a broadside ringing in his ears, shaking the timbers of the ship and blossoming into an orange glow on billows of smoke.

Again he was in Salem on a cold November day, out on the water of the harbor, pulling in a fishing line which cut into his swollen hands. He awoke from this fantasy, shivering from ague. And then his uncle, Peter Treegate, stood before him, looming over him like Goliath, his legs astride, shouting his name over and over again. The shouting continued, but the image of his uncle turned first into a bear, then into a leopard and finally into a swirling green mass.

He tried to open his eyes but the eyelashes were closed by pus. In a little while, however, he got them open and the real world came slowly back into focus. He could see the bush with the bright red flowers and beyond it the moldering wall of the church. The church wall was in shadow. He knew that it was late in the day, but what day he did not know. He could hear footsteps nearby and a heavy rustling sound. Then the bush with the red flowers shook, some of the branches were thrust aside and Mama Amelie appeared. She gave a cry on seeing him and shuffled to him, and Manly, sick, weak, his heart throbbing with fever, was glad to see her. She scolded him in a stream of patois, meanwhile touching his face and neck with her worn black fingers, and then disappeared.

It occurred to Manly that she had gone for help, and if he wanted to escape, now was his last chance. But he had neither the strength nor the desire to do so. Of all things, he wanted to be away from the church and the graveyard, and so he longed for Mama Amelie to return. She seemingly had to go all the way to the harbor for help, for she was some time getting back. She returned with Gubu. Gubu smelled heavily of rum and tobacco. His eyes were bloodshot and Mama Amelie was scolding him, so he was in a bad humor. But when he saw Manly he stopped grumbling and, picking him up with ease, flung him over his shoulder and carried him back to the brig *Constance*.

There Mama Amelie put him in the stern cabin (which was Gubu's cabin) and set about cleaning him up and ministering to him. She washed him, put clean clothes on him and cupped him with a little tin mug, and she laid fresh banana leaves over his eyes and poured a little green oil obtained from the fat of the turtles into his ears.

She also rubbed his throat with this oil and gave him a small amount of seawater to drink. She put his feet in a tub of hot brine and then she put him in a bunk and piled clothing on him until the sweat poured off him in rivulets. She lit a charcoal fire in the cabin and kept it burning so that the place was as hot as an oven, and when Manly protested that she would kill him, she said she was making it uncomfortable so as to drive the devils out of him. The worse he felt, the sooner he would get better. This treatment went on with minor alterations and additions for three days. On the third day Mama Amelie made Manly drink quantities of what she called *"eau blanc"*—white water—which had a bitter, dry taste. It proved a powerful emetic, and when he had drunk all he could, he was so weak he thought he would surely die. But to his surprise he felt very much better a day later, and enormously hungry. This time, however, Mama Amelie gave him only bland food in the form of a paste made of the pounded root of cassava. He ate this for two days before he was allowed his first taste of meat. At the end of a week he was up and about again, conscious that he owed his life to Mama Amelie.

During his illness, whenever he opened his eyes, Mama Amelie was there. When he first saw her, he thought her as ugly and fearful-looking as a human being could be. Now he could not see the ugliness. There was a lot of mischief in her old brown eyes, and the wrinkled skin and toothless mouth were really just a disguise for a willful, bold child. Toward the end of his illness Mama Amelie brought Manly a looking glass, and in it he saw his wasted cheeks and the dark circles around his eyes and was horrified. Mama Amelie then looked in the mirror herself and cackled with laughter, as if she were a little girl who had disguised herself successfully as an old woman. She grimaced at the image in the mirror and put out her tongue at herself and laughed again, and then, solemn for a moment, she found a bedraggled feather from Gubu's parrot and put it in the turban she always wore. Then she looked at Manly and something warned him not to laugh.

"Pretty," he said, and she was enormously pleased and stopped making faces at herself in the mirror.

Little by little he learned what had happened since he had run away. Gubu had sold his cargo and divided the money up among his crew, who had by now spent the greater part of it ashore. He had not had to provision the ship, but he had taken on four tons of gunpowder and ten of shot for the ship's guns, for in making a search of her stores he found she was short of both these. He was planning on going cruising "on the account" southward through the West Indian Islands.

"If he's taken, he'll be hung," said Manly.

"Why should he be taken?" countered Mama Amelie. "All through these islands, ships attack ships. French ships attack British ships. British ships attack French ships. They both attack any merchant ships they see and take off the crew. Why should it be right for them and wrong for Gubu? The captains of the big English and French ships get rich doing this. Why can they do it and go free, but if Gubu does it he will be hanged? You have any answer for that?"

"No," said Manly. "I don't have an answer. The English and the French captains have their governments behind them. But Gubu has no one behind him. If he wants to go sailing 'on the account,' he should get some government behind him."

The thought of a government supporting a former slave caused Mama Amelie great amusement. She told Gubu about it and Gubu was not so amused. He thought it was a fine idea and came to talk it over with Manly. Manly was still in the aft cabin. He would be glad to move out, but Mama Amelie had decided he was to stay there, and Gubu had come to accept his company. That he shared the captain's cabin gave him a position of quasi-authority among the crew.

"How do I get these papers?" asked Gubu.

The problem was far beyond Manly's experience, but he hazarded a guess. "I expect that you ask the governor of an island," he said. "If you went to a French island and asked the governor for papers, he might give them to you," he added. He wanted to get to a French island.

"You think I am a fool?" asked Gubu. "If I went to a French island, the governor would take my ship."

"What about Haiti?" asked Manly. "If there is a governor there, you could get papers from him." Gubu did not want to sail to Port-au-Prince, the Haitian capital, to get papers. The upshot of the discussion was that he went ashore and found the mayor of Port-au-Paix and browbeat him into giving him a letter, with a seal attached, permitting him to seize ships of the "enemies of Haiti." The seal was actually the seal of the old French government, now used as a weight in a ramshackle grocery store run by the mayor. It was very impressive, however, and Gubu had found some green sealing wax, on which the seal was impressed, with a piece of red ribbon dangling from it. It looked splendid, and when he had this paper, he called his crew together, showed it to them and made them all swear allegiance to the government of Haiti. He ran up the Haitian flag on the brig's main peak, gave everybody a glass of rum and set sail in an hour. He was so pleased with himself he fired one of the brig's carronades as he cleared the harbor mouth.

The gun, however, had been loaded with roundshot, which hissed ashore, knocking down a coconut palm, but otherwise doing no damage. It was a spirited departure and the brig was loudly cheered as she rounded the harbor mole and plunged into the blue seas beyond. Her home port had been changed from Bristol, England, to Port-au-Paix, Haiti. Gubu had given up wearing his French Chausseur's coat, which was rather worn, and now had a fine buff coat with red facings and silver buttons, belonging to a colonel of the Duke of Orléans's regiment.

He also had a laced hat and a pair of dragoon's riding boots, which, however, hurt his feet. He told the helmsman to sail westward, but would give no further course until he had consulted with Mama Amelie. Mama Amelie opened a little skin bag containing some knucklebones, one of them colored scarlet, and having shaken these in her hands, rolled them on the deck. She rolled them four times and the red knucklebone always rolled farther than the others and to the right. So she said they should sail south toward Martinique, and the ship's head, following the dictates of this extraordinary navigation, was accordingly set in that direction.

# 18

MANLY regained his health rapidly as *Constance* sailed south and west down the long chain of the Antilles. He also gained a new position on board—that of gunnery officer. This came about without any desire on his part but as a result of the complete incompetence of the crew in handling the ship's guns. At gun practice they put an overcharge of powder in one, so that it burst and killed a man and badly wounded two others. They neglected to put wadding behind the shot, so that with the roll of the ship the roundshot fell out of the barrel of the gun. And they fired one piece without ensuring that the breechings were secure, so that in recoiling, the gun charged backwards across the deck, smashing into the opposite gunwale and nearly killing another man. Even the men from Jamaica, merchant sailors all of them, had little or no gunnery experience.

Manly, on the other hand, had had plenty of gun training on *Leopard*. In fact, he had had gun training twice a day for three months, so it evolved that he knew more about guns than any man on board. Gubu decided then that he should be gunnery officer and the crew was to obey him in all matters pertaining to the ship's armament. Manly was familiar with the frigate's long twenties and the shorter-range thirty-two-pounder carronades. The brig's guns were very much lighter—nine-pounders in her main battery and a long eighteen as a chase gun forward, with four eighteen-pounder carronades on the poop aft. Manly insisted that he did not know enough to be in charge, but since everybody aboard knew less than he, that still made him the expert.

The nine-pounders being about one-half the size of the frigate's twenty-pounders, he decided they should receive but half the powder. For the eighteen-pounders he made up cartridges only slightly smaller than those for the frigate's main broadside.

He found to his horror that the gunpowder was stored in a hold close to the keel, with general ship's stores all about. Hardly anybody ever came down here, but one day he saw Mama Amelie rummaging around among the barrels of powder, smoking her stub of a black pipe. He asked for bulkheads to be erected to make a separate hold for the powder, with a lamp behind a piece of glass as was done on *Leopard*.

Strictest orders were given that nobody was to go into the powder hold smoking a pipe. Since Mama Amelie seemed incapable of going anywhere without her pipe, she was forbidden to go into the powder hold at all.

The men did not challenge Manly in these matters, being content to leave everything concerning the guns to him despite his age. He held gun practice daily for a week, just running the guns in and out and going through all the needed motions for loading and swabbing them. The crew joined readily enough to start with, but then they grew careless and contemptuous and took to skylarking during gun drill. So Manly let the gun drill go, for he was too young to establish discipline.

There were many charts aboard of the West Indian Islands, the South American mainland and the British Isles. Manly found them in the galley, where Mama Amelie was using them to light the stove. Gubu knew vaguely that they were "charts," but he could not read the writing on them. Manly showed him Martinique, toward which they were headed and which Gubu knew well by sight. He showed him the mountains on the island and the ridges of the mountains extending down the peninsula and thrusting into the sea. He showed him the main town of Saint Pierre, on the northwest corner of the island at the foot of the vast volcano Mount Pelée, which thrust four thousand feet into the sky.

"Eh, eh," said Gubu, amazed that so much could be obtained from the insignificant marks on the chart. He would not be satisfied until Manly had gone through all the other charts aboard and identified each one and named its principal features. He no longer glowered and grumbled at the boy, and let him pet the blue-and-yellow parrot on which he set such store. Gubu believed that the parrot was the source of all his good fortune. He insisted that the next time they took a prize the parrot should have its share.

Bad as was the gun drill aboard *Constance,* the discipline in the management of the ship was perhaps even worse. No regular watches were kept. When the helmsman wanted relief, he just called for someone to take the wheel from him. When a sail had to be trimmed, or sails had to be taken down, everybody bore a hand. When the lookout on the foretop wanted relief, he came down and asked someone else to go up. There were times when, nobody feeling particularly inclined to work, no lookout was kept.

Manly's plan to escape having misfired in Haiti, he decided that he would try again at Martinique, which, being French, might provide him with a haven. He did not really know what the relationship was between the United States and France, though he had heard his uncle denounce the French roundly on several occasions. But he had heard others say that Mr. Jefferson favored the French and that the French had promised not to impress American seamen and to respect the rights of American ships. He had become fond of Mama Amelie, and fond too, to a degree, of Gubu, who was certainly the most incompetent but lucky pirate imaginable. But his determination to escape was not lessened by this, and he hid some provisions in a safe place and put with them a pistol, a bag of shot and a small horn of powder in case these should be needed when he got ashore.

The brig skirted Puerto Rico, slipped through the Virgin Islands, and off Saint Eustatius took its first prize.

This was a small schooner flying Dutch colors and carrying a cargo of salted hides. She was armed only with one nine-pounder and surrendered without a fight. Gubu searched her, hoping for something more valuable than the hides, and then, having relieved the captain of the ship's store of money (amounting to three hundred guilders), he let the schooner go.

The schooner went in to Saint Eustatius and reported to the governor that she had been stopped by a brig flying Haitian colors. The governor sent a fast boat to the British colony of Antigua with the news of the pirate, and the governor at Antigua informed the captain of the sloop of war *Panther* preparing for sea in an English harbor. *Panther* was headed south down the Leeward and Windward Islands on the same kind of work as *Constance*. But *Panther* was a warship and could claim that she had a right to stop vessels and seize them if carrying contraband. Contraband was anything which was forbidden for a neutral nation to supply to Britain's enemies, and since Britain's enemies at this time embraced half of Europe, *Panther* could stop and search any vessel with impunity. She found when she got to sea that a number of the vessels she stopped had already been searched by the new Haitian pirate, and so a hunt for Gubu and *Constance* was commenced and had soon spread through the whole chain of islands. Twice *Panther* had *Constance* in sight and gave chase, but the brig was the faster vessel and got away each time. Manly, however, was desperately afraid of capture, which for him, if he was identified, would mean a flogging as a deserter as well as a return to the gun deck of some frigate or man-of-war, if he survived the flogging.

Then one day, in a dying wind, four miles off the island of Martinique, *Panther* came upon them. *Constance,* trying to make her way to the westward side of the island, had fallen into the lee of the vast volcano Mount Pelée. *Panther,* farther offshore, still had the wind. Indeed, the line of the wind, marked by whitecaps, could be plainly seen on the water only half a mile to seaward. *Constance* was trapped, for she could not maneuver. She could not outfight the sloop of war, which had much heavier guns. But Gubu could not believe that his luck had deserted him, for he still had his blue-and-yellow parrot.

"We will get the wind," he asserted, while his crew lined the bulwarks in dismay as *Panther* came nearer. "Something will happen. We will escape." He brought the parrot on deck and chained it to the ship's rail to encourage the crew. Mama Amelie had not his faith in the bird.

"Better to take to the boats," she said. "We can get to shore. Otherwise, they will hang us." But Gubu ordered the guns loaded and run out. *Panther* now opened fire, the shot from her twelve-pounders plumping down around *Constance,* but without damage. The brig replied, somewhat ridiculously, and the broadside from her light guns had a sharp high crack which sent thousands of birds flying up from the thick forests at the foot of the nearby volcano. *Constance* was lying motionless in utterly calm water, so her aim was more reliable, and one or two of her shots plumped into the sides of the sloop of war but did not cripple her. The warship tacked to bring another broadside to bear and this time did better. The brig's bowsprit was snapped off and her main topmast came dangling down, the topsail still stretched on the yard like a broken wing.

That was enough for the crew. They ran for the boats, tumbling them into the water and jumping into them. One boat pushed off so fast that the men aboard forgot the oars and drifted helplessly away from the brig's side. They begged Gubu to throw the oars to them, but he was in a towering rage and fired his pistol over their heads. *Panther* now fired again. She had the range right and several shots plumped into the topsides of the brig. One, speeding across the deck in a flat trajectory, tore the gunwale out of the brig and plopped into the oarless boat. No one was hit, but the bottom was stove and the boat started to sink.

At that moment miraculously the wind came up. The remaining sails on *Constance* filled, and with no one at her helm, she fell off the wind and ran down on her crew struggling in the water. These swarmed aboard as Gubu took the wheel. Enough of the bowsprit was left to set a staysail and jib, and as the wind piped up and filled the sails, the parrot let out a loud, jeering squawk, the crew cheered and the brig gained speed.

One other boat was still over the brig's side, trailing behind her on a long painter. At the sight of it Manly made up his mind. He paused only to pick up the pistol and other stores he had put aside, and while everyone was scurrying about the deck trimming sail, he pulled the gig up to the brig's counter and lowered these into it and then got in himself.

Nobody saw him but Mama Amelie. She ran to the transom, but he had already cast off. She shrieked to Gubu but he, determined to escape the sloop of war, paid her no notice. She screeched to Manly to come back, and then, in a kind of frenzy of despair, jumped or fell overboard after him. *Panther* fired another broadside, but the wind had come around to the north now and it was brisk, so *Constance* was an accelerating target. The broadside raised a dozen white splashes in the water but left *Constance* untouched.

Manly saw *Panther* swing around to follow the brig, which was already a quarter of a mile off. Between him and the brig was Mama Amelie, a pathetic little bundle of clothes in the water. For a second, Manly considered leaving her there to swim ashore by herself or be picked up by the brig later, if by some miracle it should escape the sloop of war. But he could not do this. He owed Mama Amelie too much, and so he rowed to her and picked her up. She got into the boat quickly and started scolding him right away. She was so angry she beat him on the head with her withered fist and pulled his hair. And then her fury was gone and she sat quietly in the stern of the boat. After a while Manly realized that she was crying.

"What is the matter, Mama Amelie?" he asked.

"Gubu will be hanged," she said. He could not comfort her.

# 19

M ANLY now had a choice of rowing directly to the shore,
landing on Martinique and making his way across the
island to the principal town of Saint Pierre on the western
coast, or rowing around the northern shore to the town.
During the approach to the island on *Constance* he had
studied the chart many times and reckoned that the sea
distance to Saint Pierre must be twenty miles and the land
distance, across the northern end of the island, about
twelve. But the land road crossed the flank of that great
volcano which had deprived *Constance* of wind. He
doubted the road would be much more than a goat path
and wondered if Mama Amelie would be able to make
the climb. So he decided to row around the coast to Saint
Pierre, setting the small spritsail, with which the gig was
equipped, if the wind served.

He bent to his oars then, and the gig moved readily

through the inshore water. The brig had managed, despite her crippled spars, to draw ahead of the British sloop, and both had disappeared around a point of the island some distance to the south. They heard two further broadsides, which came to them like distant thunder, and then silence. Then there was a much heavier series of explosions and again silence. After a little while, they saw a dark column of smoke rising from behind the point which hid the brig and the British warship from them. They guessed that *Constance* had been taken and set on fire, and that conclusion seemed confirmed when there came a very heavy explosion from beyond the point and a dense column of smoke rose up in the air.

"Gubu may have got ashore," said Manly.

"He was too stupid," said Mama Amelie dully. "They will hang him. If he had only stayed with his little sloop, he would be alive and happy now."

"And I would have been drowned," said Manly.

"Who cares about you?" snapped Mama Amelie, suddenly enraged. "You are bad luck for everybody, too. You and that parrot. I should kill you now." She was in a fury and snatched up the pistol which was lying in the bottom of the boat. She pointed it directly at Manly's head and, before he could stop her, pulled the trigger. Nothing happened. She lowered the pistol and stared at him. He snatched it from her and threw it into the bow of the boat where she could not get at it. Angry as she was before, she was entirely calm now, looking at him, however, with superstitious awe.

"You have a great power," she said simply.

"The priming was damp," he snapped at her.

"That is your power. Water will never permit anything to harm you. I picked you up out of the sea which would not harm you, and the sea damped the priming of the pistol. And if you had not taken to the sea in this little boat, you would be hung now with Gubu."

"Gubu may not be hung at all," Manly said. He was very angry with her for trying to shoot him, and yet he felt sorry for her. Suddenly a thought occurred to him. "Who was Gubu to you?" he asked.

"Gubu was my son," she said.

They rowed in silence for the next hour. The land slipped gradually away to the westward until they had changed course sufficiently to make some use of the north wind. Manly unrolled the spritsail and set it on its little stumpy mast in the eye of the boat. He had to use an oar in a rowlock over the transom to steer, but the gig sped along handsomely, making little tinkling noises as the small waves splashed against its side.

They went on like this for another hour, covering a sea distance of four miles in that time, and then came to a point of land which jutted far out into the sea and around which they had to row. Once this was negotiated, however, they had passed the northernmost point of the island, and their course being now southerly down the western side, they had a fair wind and made good speed.

The sun set and with it went the wind. Manly took to the oars again and headed the boat in close to the shore. The water here seemed to be enormously deep, and all was as calm as a lake. As the sun set, the water turned from deep blue to pale blue, then to grey and then to black. Phosphorescence boiled around the oars in whirls of golden light. Fish streaked through the black water like blazing rockets. The land and the two in the boat seemed to be floating in the sky, with the blazing stars below and about them.

All day Manly had eaten nothing. Now he remembered the provisions he had put aboard wrapped in a piece of cloth. He lay down the oars and asked Mama Amelie to get the food. It consisted of fruit and boiled yams, but he ate only sparingly. Mama Amelie meanwhile took the oars. Old as she was, she had surprising strength and endurance. She stood up at the oars and rowed facing forward, and at the same time hummed a sad little tune which had at the end of each verse a recurring phrase that Manly could not quite catch.

"What song are you singing?" he asked.

"It is about two creatures," she said. "One was called Always and the other Never."

"What happened to them?"

"They were joined together and became the first human beings," said Mama Amelie. "When you are grown up, you will understand that."

"I think I understand it now," said Manly. "We are always expecting something good and it never happens." He thought of all the things that had happened to him since he had persuaded Coffin to let him go sailing on Chesapeake Bay. If only he had stayed ashore. Indeed, if only he had not persuaded his uncle to take him on the visit to Norfolk, now he would be happily back in Salem instead of in a small boat with an old black woman off an island utterly foreign to him where even worse might be in store for him. He wondered what would happen to all the children who had made Coffin's life such a turmoil while he was alive. How terribly their lives had been changed by the decision to go for a sail on Chesapeake Bay. He remembered the four Leghorns that wouldn't lay eggs, and Coffin's complaining—"Here's me with Sue Anne screeching and thirteen children a-screaming about the place and four Leghorns that won't lay nohow and my days filled with work and no profit from it, and there's you, just a boy with no wife and no children and no work and your pocket filled with money . . ."

There was no sense in the death of Coffin, none at all. He was an entirely innocent man swept into violence not of his making. And there was no sense in Manly's being off this strange island in a small boat with an old black woman whose son had probably been hanged that morning.

He had been brought up to believe that everything made sense. His mother had held this view and his aunt held it even more strongly. "God's will makes sense of everything," was a favorite saying of hers. But Manly could not see that Coffin's death in a frigate's broadside and the hanging of Gubu (who, although he was a pirate, was curiously simple and innocent) made any sense at all. He sighed and turned to the problem of what he was to do when he got ashore.

Should he just go boldly to the French officials, say who he was, and ask to be sent back to America, since his uncle would certainly pay his passage and probably a large reward for his return? That was the obvious thing to do, but Manly suspected now that direct bold action, unplanned, often led to misfortune. He should be more cautious.

He was, after all, entirely alone—a boy in his early teens. He had no one to take his cause. He would be in an adult world which was at war, and those adults with whom he would have to deal might not be honest. They might put him in jail. They might sentence him to serve on a ship for being illegally in their country. They might sell him as a slave. Slavery flourished in Martinique, and not all slaves were black.

So he reasoned he would be taking a foolish risk to go straight to the French authorities and announce his presence on the island. If there were, by chance, an American ship in the harbor, he would be safe. But, failing that, he had to find a friend—someone who would speak for him. And the only friend he had in the world, he suddenly realized, was Mama Amelie. What ties bound her to him he did not know. But she had certainly saved his life once. And in a moment perhaps of hysteria she had chosen to stay with him instead of with her son, Gubu.

She still stood at the oars, singing her little song about "Always" and "Never."

> *"Tu m'aime, petit? C'est vrai? C'est vrai?"*
> *"Toujours, toujours. Jamais, jamais."**

The little song hung lonely in the night over the tiny boat on the dark water.

* "You love me, little one? It's true? It's true?"
  "Always, always. Never, never."

# 20

They landed the boat in the dark on a beach on the northern shore of the bay in which the town of Saint Pierre was situated. They came cautiously to the beach, which was of rough white sand, and found close to shore a tangled growth of sea grapes and tamarinds. They hauled the boat into this, turned it over and, propping one end up with an oar, made a shelter for themselves in which to pass the night.

It was a bad night for Manly. His dreams were disturbed with thoughts of his uncle and his home in Salem. He dreamed that he could see his uncle and his aunt in the great dining room of the house in Salem. He dreamed that he was, in fact, in the same room with them, calling to them. But when they looked in his direction they could not see him, nor could they hear a word he was saying. They were completely unaware of his presence.

He woke and found the night still dark and Mama Amelie wheezing in her sleep under the boat. Then he dreamed that he was lying under the boat in the thicket of sea grapes and tamarinds, and Midshipman Prynne was coming toward him with a body of seamen. He could hear his high-pitched voice and the clumping of the seamen through the brush. But he could not move a finger. He could not even call out. He was compelled by some invisible constraint to lie there while Prynne came to capture him. At last, making a mighty effort, he woke up to find the sun just clearing the top of the hills and Mama Amelie cleaning a fish with his sheath knife. She cleaned it quickly, skinned it and cut the flesh up into little chunks. Then she produced four or five small green limes which she cut in two, and she squeezed the juice over the translucent flesh of the fish. The juice immediately turned the flesh an opaque white. She passed him some on a broad banana leaf.

"Where did you get the fish?" he asked.

"A fisherman came by," she said. "Eat it."

He began with some reluctance. It tasted remarkably good. He had awakened thirsty, but when he had eaten a little of the raw fish "cooked" in lime juice, his thirst was gone.

"Did he tell you any news?" asked Manly.

"You are safe now," said Mama Amelie. "The British ship was taken yesterday."

"Taken?" cried Manly. "Impossible. Who could take her?" An idea occurred to him. "The two-decker—the *Indomptable?*"

"No French warship," said Mama Amelie. "But a French privateer, *Bonne Chance*." And she explained about Rougecroix and his heavily armed schooner. "Between the two of them—*Constance* and *Bonne Chance*—they forced the British ship to surrender."

"So Gubu is alive, then?" cried Manly.

"He is a fool, but he is alive," said Mama Amelie.

"What was the explosion we heard?" asked Manly.

"That was the British sloop," said Mama Amelie. "When she surrendered, her men got off in boats, rowed over to *Bonne Chance* and *Constance* and said she was sinking fast. But they had set a short fuse in her powder hold and blew her up."

This was good news for Mama Amelie but not so good for Manly. For the second time he had tried to get away from Gubu and *Constance* and had failed, though he still had a chance to evade Gubu if he acted immediately.

He made up his mind in a moment. "Mama Amelie," he said, "I'm going. You'll never get me back on board *Constance*. I'll find some place to hide on this island. Or I will go to jail on this island. But I won't go back to *Constance*. I am going to find a ship somehow that will take me back to my home."

"Gubu will take you back to your home," said Mama Amelie calmly.

"Gubu?" cried Manly. "All he will ever do is have me hung for a pirate."

"No, he won't," she said. "You come with me to Gubu."

"No," said Manly. "I'm going. Now." He rose and was

about to turn on his heel and stride off when she leveled the pistol at him.

"It won't fire," he said.

"Are you sure?" she asked mockingly.

"It is the same priming," said Manly. "It is still damp."

"Then go," said Mama Amelie.

It took all the resolution he possessed to turn on his heel, but he did. He took two steps away from her and heard the dull "click" as she cocked the hammer. He took another step and there was a roaring explosion, and he felt the ball whistle past his ear. He ran then, thoroughly frightened, and when he had gone some distance, he turned around. Mama Amelie was kneeling on the beach and moaning, the pistol thrown from her, her head in her hands. He stopped and stared at her, irresolute, and then something so completely lonely and comfortless about her moved him to come back.

She looked up at him and there was not a tear in her eyes. In fact, she was laughing. "Ah-ha," she said. "You see. I am a witch. You know of any woman, old like me, who can shoot at a man and have him come back to her in less than a minute? Now we will go to see Gubu and he will take you to America. He will do it because I will tell him to."

Manly, picking up the pistol, could still have run off. But his emotions had been subjected to such a series of shocks—stark terror, pity and then derision—all within the space of a minute or two, that he was for a while incapable of independent action. He didn't for a moment believe that Gubu would take him to America. But he couldn't, at this point, leave Mama Amelie.

"Promise me one thing," he said. "Promise that if I go back with you to Gubu you will not try to stop me leaving again."

"Gubu will take you home," she repeated.

"I don't believe that," said Manly.

"Until you came along," snapped Mama Amelie, "Gubu, who is a grown man, had done everything I told him. Who are you to tell me he won't obey me now? Come, help me with the boat."

Manly helped her get the boat down into the water again, largely because too much had happened too suddenly for him to think clearly about his problem. If Mama Amelie was not a witch, she had certainly gotten him completely confused, and to that extent it could be said that she had cast a spell over him. It was still early morning and so there wasn't a whisper of wind on the water of the bay. Manly took the oars and started rowing, and in an hour they were in sight of Saint Pierre. His heart sank as he saw the familiar lines of the *Constance* at anchor, with Gubu on her stern, his blue-and-gold parrot on his shoulder. In twenty minutes they were alongside, and Gubu picked his mother up bodily off the deck in his huge arms.

"But you came back to me, Mama Amelie," he kept saying, as if this was something beyond belief. And then he roared for rum, and a pannikin of the white fiery fluid was brought and Mama Amelie sucked it down like milk. Gubu showed no animosity toward Manly for having deserted the ship. He was scarcely in a position to do so, since the whole of his crew had done the same in the ridiculous battle with the British sloop of war.

When matters had become a little quieter, however, he gave Manly a knowing look and said, "I got some news for you. You going back to your home. And I gonna take you there."

This announcement, confirming the statement—indeed, the prophecy—of Mama Amelie, completely dumfounded Manly. Indeed, it dumfounded Mama Amelie, who choked on the second pannikin of rum which had been handed to her.

"Why didn't you say when you first came aboard that you are a friend of Theophilous Jones?" demanded Gubu.

"Theophilous Jones?" echoed Manly. Indeed, he had forgotten all about the mysterious black with his multitudinous connections, not readily defined, in seaports throughout the world.

"That man sent a special message about you to a lot of people down here sailing on the account," said Gubu. "In fact, before I rose to command this brig, I carried a message from Mr. Jones to Captain Jean Rougecroix on *Bonne Chance* about you."

"What did the message say?" asked Manly, his heart pounding.

"I can't read," said Gubu. "But that message said, according to Captain Rougecroix, that anybody who brings you back to America, safe and sound, will get ten thousand dollars in silver. And that's got to be me."

"When did you find this out?" asked Manly.

"When I told Captain Rougecroix about you stealing my gig and running away during the battle." He reflected on the desertion for a moment and was angry. "I was the only one left on this brig," he stormed.

"You and the parrot," said Mama Amelie. "And the parrot had all the brains." She gave a cackling laugh in which the parrot, to Gubu's annoyance, joined. Manly had one or two further questions. "Did you get the message for Captain Rougecroix directly from Theophilous Jones?" he asked, for he was surprised at the thought of Gubu's tiny sloop making a journey from Chesapeake to the West Indies.

"How Mr. Jones gets his messages about the place is his secret," said Gubu, and with that Manly had to be content. There was, however, one further surprise for him in that day full of surprise when all the misfortunes of the past few months were reversed.

This came when *Constance* began to discharge the prisoners from the British sloop of war who had been confined in her hold until arrangements for their detention could be made ashore. The third person to come out of the hatch was none other than Midshipman Prynne. He recognized Manly immediately. "Turned pirate, eh, Treegate? One day you'll swing for it," he said.

"Shut up, you fool," said one of the other British officers. But Gubu had heard and he didn't like the word "pirate."

"I got a Haiti paper," he said. "You got an English paper and I got a Haiti paper and we both doing the same thing. How come I'm a pirate and you're not?" He turned to Manly. "You know him?" he said, indicating Prynne.

For answer, Manly showed Gubu the lines of the rope often laid across his back by Prynne. They still showed white on his tanned torso. Gubu had the same lines, black and cut deeper. He reached to a belaying pin and threw Manly a short piece of knotted rope.

"Get him off my ship," he said.

But Prynne was gone before Manly even raised the rope. He darted through the other prisoners, and in his hurry to get over the side into the boat, he fell into the water and was fished out by the boatman. Mama Amelie watched him and the others being rowed ashore and then said, "He's like a mapapi—a snake. Next time you see that one, don't talk. Kill him." She meant it.

# 21

THE Christmas dinner, eaten at midday, was over in the big dining room of Peter Treegate's house in Salem. The servants had removed the meat and vegetable dishes, and Peter Treegate, looking grimmer and a trifle older than he had at his birthday in midsummer, had asked permission of his guests to open and read a message that arrived at just that moment from the city of Washington. The guests pretended to chatter among themselves while Peter Treegate broke the seal of the Department of State that was on the back of the letter. He glanced at the signature, saw the word "Madison" and read:

"Dear Mr. Treegate, I have now received definite news about the fate of your nephew Manly Treegate. My information comes both from our minister in London and from the British naval authorities in Halifax, Nova Scotia, the latter source reporting through our own maritime department.

"It gives me the greatest pain to have to report that the boy was lost overboard in the West Indies during an engagement between the frigate *Leopard* and a French two-decker, *Indomptable*. This engagement took place a few miles to the north of the Kingdom of Haiti, in October last, and no word of the boy having been received from any source whatever since then, it is presumed that he is dead. The British Admiralty have indicated that on the submission of proof of the boy's American citizenship in proper form they might consider payment . . ." Mr. Treegate read no further.

His wife, Nancy, at the other end of the table, took her attention from an anecdote of Mrs. Abigail Adams (for the guests were the same as had sat at the table on Mr. Treegate's birthday) to glance at her husband. She saw from the set of his face that the news was bad. But she had been brought up to tremendous self-control and knew how to wait. She watched her husband fold the letter and stare with unseeing eyes at the place before him.

"Mr. Treegate," she said, "the children."

He was startled and looked at her. "Madam?" he inquired.

"The children, Mr. Treegate," she said. "They are waiting to join us for dessert." He closed his eyes momentarily, for the memory of that family custom was now so painful. Then, because it meant so much to the children and to her, he said, "Of course. Let them come in. I am sure our guests will indulge us."

There was a murmur of consent and pleasure from around the table and Mrs. Treegate nodded to the servant standing at the double door. The door was opened and for a moment there was only the sound of a scuffle in the darkness of the hall beyond. And then into the room came a tall boy, dressed in seaman's clothes but of good quality, his skin as dark as the shell of a hazelnut. He walked boldly into the room, his chin held a little high, and when he was within a few feet of the table he stopped, made a short bow and said, "Happy Christmas, Uncle. I trust you will not find me an unwelcome gift." Peter Treegate stared, unbelieving, and then there was a little cry from the head of the table and his wife, Nancy, all her reserve gone, rushed down and clasped Manly in her arms.

"God has heard the prayers of the least of his servants," she said, the tears streaming from her eyes.

Then a great tumult broke out—chairs were pushed back and everybody crowded around Manly, the men shaking his hand and thumping him on the back and the women smothering him in hugs, oblivious to the effect on the silks and laces with which they were adorned.

When all had at last settled down into some sense of order, Manly said to his uncle, "Sir, I beg leave to introduce to you a lady who twice saved my life and twice tried to shoot me. Without her, however, I would not be here."

He turned to the door and held out a hand, and Mama Amelie came in. She had parted with her little stub of a pipe for the occasion and Theophilous Jones had clad her in a lovely gown of watered-blue silk.

She was a small black figure, oddly proud, but quite

out of place it seemed, and the ladies gasped and looked at each other, uncertain what to do. Then Mrs. Nancy Treegate pushed past her nephew and, going to her with outstretched hands, said, "My dear, please come and sit by me. You are one of us and will be for the rest of your days."

That midday Christmas dinner lasted into supper and beyond supper, until the children all had been sent to bed and Manly had told every detail of his story and answered everybody's questions.

But when it was done, Mr. Treegate summed it all up for him. "You were the *Leopard*'s prey," he said, "and as matters now stand, we are all of us the *Leopard*'s prey and will be until we arm ourselves and boldly take our own part."

Colonel Beddington of the Sixth Regiment of Foot, back from the Ohio frontier, raised his glass and begged leave to propose a toast.

"Here's to a reckoning with the *Leopard,* and all beasts of prey," he said. The toast was drunk with enthusiasm.